Golden Hood

Midnight Empire: New Dawn, Book 1

Annabel Chase

Red Palm Press LLC

Chapter One

I balanced on the thick branch of a black locust tree and waited. Any minute now.

"I've got a burr stuck in my calf," Hattie complained from the ground below.

Somebody shushed her. Probably Hugo.

The hum of two engines cut through the silence, and I moved to a crouched position, careful to maintain my balance on the branch.

"Here they come," Bear whispered.

"Gee, and here I thought someone was petting a large cat," Victor shot back.

"Sounds like their wheels are misaligned," Scarlet whispered.

Hugo's fierce shush ripped through the clearing. The sound of the engines grew louder, and the vehicles entered the clearing in a single file line, too wide to enter the space side by side. The 4x4s, commonly known as 'Beasts,' had been designed for tough terrain, but what passed as tough terrain in a pre-Eternal Night world was vastly different from the current reality. Still, the vehicles held their own against The Wild's topography. Misaligned wheels or not, I hoped we could salvage one. We were in need of a replacement.

From his position behind a tree, Hugo tossed a ball of twine into the clearing. The ball looked innocent enough but had been heavily coated in one of his potions. Sometimes I wondered how talented the wizard would be now if he'd finished his education. Regardless, we were fortunate to have him as part of our crew.

Magic exploded from the device, filling the clearing with orange smoke. Flesh turned to fur, and the rest of the crew pounced. As the smoke cleared, I saw that the vehicles had tipped to opposing sides. The werewolves had dragged four vampires from their seats and fought until the vampires were rendered unconscious. All except the fifth one, of course. The tax collector himself was off limits. The poor guy seemed oblivious to the fact that he'd been deliberately spared. He climbed to his feet and ran toward the bosom of the forest—toward me, his pace slowed by the heavy sack he was desperate to carry.

From several branches above him, I opened my hand and released a blinding light. The vampire staggered backward in surprise and dropped the sack.

"Turn off the flashlight," he yelled.

I closed my hand before I could do any real damage to the vampire. My crew swooped in and grabbed the fallen loot before he recovered. By the time his eyesight adjusted, the rangers were still unconscious, and my crew was gone.

I pulled up the hood of my cloak and stepped across the forest canopy to another branch. It wasn't as sturdy as it appeared and the bark cracked, prompting the tax collector to look up.

"You!" His tone made it sound like a swear word.

Even shrouded in darkness, I was sure the vampire head permanently impaled on one of my arrows didn't escape his notice.

"Lord Doran will hear about this!"

"I should hope so, or he might think you're to blame."

"It's his money you stole!" the vampire continued, shaking an angry fist.

"No, it isn't. It's money he took by force from people who need it more than he does."

The vampire bristled. "I didn't take it by force. Tax collection is part of any civilized community."

"You think The Wild is civilized? The answer's right there in the name. The vampires only take care of themselves. Everybody else is food or sport. Do you think we should pay for the privilege?"

He scowled. "You should talk, Hooded One. You murder vampires simply for doing their job, and you carry a head of my kind like a trophy. If that isn't sport, I don't know what it is."

"It isn't sport for us. It's survival," I said. "Take one of the Beasts and return to your lord and master. We'll keep the other in exchange for your life."

Uncertainty flashed in his eyes. He seemed concerned that it might be a trick.

"If I wanted you dead, you'd be dead," I told him. "Go on before I change my mind."

Grunting, he returned to the clearing and pushed one of the Beasts to an upright position. Then he climbed into the driver's seat where he spared a final glance at his unconscious companions before fleeing the scene.

I waited until the sound of the engine faded to push the second Beast onto its four oversized tires and slide behind the wheel. I drove through the forest, bouncing over protruding roots and plowing through bushes. I knew the vampire wouldn't follow. He was a tax collector, not a fighter. He'd simply report the loss to Lord Doran and face the consequences. Knowing what I did of Lord Doran, they would be brutal.

Good.

Along the way, I noticed a cluster of trees had grown brown and brittle. The magic that had once infused them was slowly draining away. Lord Doran had made a grave mistake when he destroyed the coven. That one decision had doomed The Wild to devastation. Without magic, what remained would eventually die. My grandmother would turn in her grave if she had one.

There were no markers to guide me to the hideout. Nothing that could give our position away to the enemy. If you couldn't find your way, then you didn't belong there. Lord Doran and his minions had tried many times to root us out, even using werewolves at one point, but we'd managed to evade him every time. Usually because the minions to which he entrusted the job were more inclined to support us than turn us over to the authorities. Even mercenaries drew a line in the dirt when it came to me.

I stopped the Beast half a mile from the hideout and walked the rest of the way on foot, on the off chance Doran's rangers were able to track the tire marks. It wasn't a major concern; The Wild excelled at keeping secrets.

The hideout consisted of a campfire, storage containers, an outhouse, and tree houses camouflaged by our surroundings. We'd built the houses as high as we could to avoid detection from the ground. We'd had to steal most of the materials, so the project had taken longer than it should have as a result, but at least we had a place to call home.

"Here she is. The woman of the hour," Hugo

announced. The wizard was average height with thinning brown hair and eyes slightly too close together, but not so much that he appeared cross-eyed.

I took a sweeping bow.

"Did he try to fight you?" Hugo asked with amusement.

"No, he felt the need to say a few words so he could tell Doran he resisted."

"I almost felt sorry for him," Scarlet said. Short and stocky with a tangle of brown curls that framed her face, the werewolf was my number two most of the time, although Hugo would happily claim the spot if I let him.

Bonnie grimaced. "Why would you ever feel sorry for a vampire? I would've been perfectly content for Aster to obliterate all five of them with the wave of a hand."

Victor looked at her. "Then who would deliver the message to Doran?"

"The tax collector's head on a spike would be a more effective message," Bonnie said. She tucked a strand of blond hair behind her ear. "Not that anyone cares about my opinion."

"I don't use magic to kill," I reminded her.

Bonnie shot me a scalding look. "Oh, yes. Shooting them with poison arrows is so much more humane."

"We only kill in self-defense. That's the rule." If we killed without provocation, then we were no better than monsters. I wasn't opposed to fear and intimidation tactics, however. The Hooded One persona had become an effective weapon against our vampire overlords.

"You let him take one of the Beasts?" Bear asked.

Tyson gave his arm a light punch. "She can't drive two at once now, can she?"

"One Beast was the plan we agreed to," I said.

Victor's hand shot in the air. "I call dibs on this one."

"You've got to be kidding," Scarlet scoffed. "You're the reason we need another one."

"What choice did I have? The bridge was out," Victor countered. "I thought I could make it across."

Scarlet shook her head. "Unless that river is an inch high, I don't know why you thought was an option."

"Let's not breathe new life into that argument," I told them. My gaze landed on the sacks the crew had stolen. There was the one dropped by the tax collector, as well as two more taken from the Beasts that my cohorts had grabbed.

Hugo sifted through the contents of one of the sacks, prompting Scarlet to smack his hand away. "What do you think you're doing?"

Hugo ignored her and continued nosing through the items. "What's this?"

"Not yours. That's what it is." Scarlet tried to swipe the object from his grasp, but Hugo was taller and held it out of reach.

"Hugo, we're giving all this back to the people who gave it," I said.

"I'm keeping this one," Hugo said, holding up an empty potion bottle. "I ruined the last one in order to make the smoke bomb."

"And a very lovely smoke bomb it was," Bear said. "Hats off to you, sir."

Hugo tipped an imaginary hat at the werewolf. "If I'm going to be an outlaw, I might as well do it in style."

I smiled. "The tax collector told me to turn off my flashlight."

"Better that than the truth," Scarlet murmured.

Hugo regarded the sacks. "Not a shabby haul for a

bunch of peasants. No wonder Doran insists on collecting taxes."

I clenched my jaw. "Don't call them that. It's demeaning." The humans that lived in the surrounding villages were at the mercy of the vampires and had been ever since the Eternal Night began. More accurately, we were all at the mercy of the Fallen, but humans had it worse because they served as the vampires' primary food source. There were rules in place to protect other species from donating blood, although they were sometimes broken without recompense.

"The villagers can't hear me, you know," Hugo said. "Too far away."

"Doesn't matter. I can hear you."

"We're better off when we rob vampires," Tyson said. "At least then we can give the people money they didn't already have. All we're doing now is returning what was taken."

I glanced up to see the werewolf's long legs dangling over the edge of a tree house. "When you scout a good mark, please feel free to share with the class. In the meantime, we'll return to the village and give back what's rightfully theirs."

"Stealing the tax collection is going to make Doran madder than a poked hornet," Tyson remarked.

"From what we know, Doran wakes up madder than a poked hornet anyway," I shot back. "So no harm done."

Tyson tossed an apple core to the ground. "You injured his rangers."

"*We* injured his rangers," Bear corrected him. "We're a team, remember?"

A bleating sound drew my attention to the edge of the clearing. A black and white goat stood there, staring at us.

"I think one of Doran's spies might've found us," Bear cracked.

"I noticed him trailing behind the tax collector. I think he was meant to be a payment," Scarlet said.

"Aw. Can we keep him?" Hattie fixed me with a pleading look. At eighteen, she was the youngest member of our crew, and sometimes it showed.

I marched over to the goat and grabbed him by the collar. "He will be returned to his rightful owner the same as everything else."

"Spoilsport," Hattie muttered.

"We could take a trip to Anchorage," Tyson suggested. "We'd find more than a few good marks there. More vampire money than Fairbanks, that's for sure."

"It's too far. Besides, I hate the city," I said.

"Then you don't have to go," Hugo said smoothly. "You don't always need to be the one in charge, you know. As Bear said, this is a team effort."

Hattie picked up a few coins that had spilled from the sack and placed them back inside. "That's not strictly true. Aster is our figurehead. If we go without her, then somebody else has to be the Hooded One."

I gripped the fabric of my signature golden cloak. "Nobody's wearing my clothes."

Hugo snorted. "We all have cloaks, Your Highness. Nobody needs yours."

"Nobody else has a golden one," Scarlet pointed out. "That's what she's known for. If it's any black hood, the vampires won't know it's us."

"Then we'll tell them," Tyson said. "Leave a calling card. Shine a few flashlights."

I rolled my eyes. "This is absurd. Stop. There's no need to head to Anchorage. It would take days. There's enough traffic through the Fairbanks area that we can support the people by staying put."

Fairbanks was a good six hours from Anchorage by car —and nobody in these parts had access to transportation, unless you counted the 4x4s and horses owned by Lord Doran. The Beast we'd stolen today was best kept in The Wild.

Hattie's eyes lit up as she spotted a shiny apple that had rolled across the clearing. "Can I eat it?" She scooped up the ripe piece of fruit. "Finders keepers, right?"

I snatched the apple from her hand before she could bite it. "What if this apple belonged to a family? No, it goes back along with everything else." I tossed the apple into the sack. "Now who's going with me?" We needed to go now before Lord Doran sent his minions after us. Soon they'd be scouring the villages for evidence of our identities.

"Doran's only going to demand the taxes be paid twice over," Bear said as he emerged from behind a tree he'd presumably been watering with his urine. He zipped his pants. "I'm beginning to think Tyson had a point."

Tyson waved from above. "Thanks, buddy."

"I agree it isn't practical, but we remain a thorn in their side, and that's all I really want," I said.

Victor cut a glance at the sacks in the clearing. "But it's the people who'll pay for your games. The same people you claim to champion."

I looked at Scarlet who shrugged.

"The more trouble we cause, the more Doran's focus is on us and not tormenting the rest of the population," I countered. "It's worthwhile."

"Admit it. You do it because you enjoy it." Bear ambled toward me wearing a mild grin. Despite the name, he wasn't a particularly large man. He'd earned the nickname by punching a bear in the face and living to tell the tale. According to Bear, he was drunk and mistook the bear for another werewolf.

I squared my shoulders. "If you love what you do, you never work a day in your life."

Hugo barked a laugh. "Who told you that?"

I pivoted to face him. "My grandmother."

The wizard fell silent. He'd known my grandmother. Everybody older than twenty had known Maya Goodfellow, or at least the name.

"I like what we do," Hattie chimed in. She was forever trying to stay on my good side. She seemed to have an unfounded fear that I'd move camp one day and leave her behind. "Besides, somebody has to keep Lord Doran Pope on his toes. If not us, then who?"

Victor lifted an axe and split a log in two. "We've seen what he does to rebels."

"If you're not interested in being a part of our merry band, then feel free to move along." Scarlet wiggled her fingers in a dismissive gesture.

Victor grinned at her. "Then who would whittle your wood?"

Scarlet laughed. "I think you've got that the wrong way 'round."

Tyson perked up. "Since when does Scarlet whittle anybody's wood?"

Victor raised his axe again. "It was a joke."

"Enough chitchat," I said. Sometimes even the most innocuous conversations erupted into a fight. Werewolves weren't exactly known for their even tempers. "Who's going to help me redistribute this sack?"

I was relieved when Hattie, Victor, and Bear volunteered. Three was good enough.

Chapter Two

We knew the tax collector had come from the village of Berthold. We'd been given a heads-up by the owner of a local pub that a date had been set, so we tracked the vampires there and prepared our ambush for their return journey.

"This goat has chewed half my shirt on the way here," Bear complained.

"He must know how good you taste," Hattie said, casting a sidelong glance at him.

"Stop flirting," I told her. "If Bonnie hears you, it'll be another Great Eruption."

"Then Bonnie needs to stop making him seem so attractive," Hattie said. "Those two kept me up half the night with her constant moaning."

Bear was unconcerned. "We're trying for a pup."

Hattie regarded him. "Do you really think now is a good time to bring a new life into the world?"

He shrugged his broad shoulders. "Now is as good a time as any."

I didn't disagree with Hattie. "It would be hard to protect a child."

"Then I guess Bonnie and I would have to make a decision at that point." He shifted the sack in his arms. "Listen, I'm not worrying about it right now. Let's build that baby first."

Hattie snorted. "It's not a Lego."

"Or a *Field of Dreams*," I added.

Bear whistled. "You had to go and reference one of my favorite movies."

"When did you ever see a movie?" I asked. From the way Bear tells it, he was born in the wilderness and never left.

"I've seen movies." He stepped over a log on the forest floor to avoid tripping. "I stayed with a family when I was younger, and they had an old DVD collection and a working player. I watched every movie they owned by the time I left."

"Why did you?" Hattie asked. "Leave, I mean."

Bear scratched the back of his neck. "Couldn't overstay my welcome."

Bear and Bonnie had been part of our crew for three years. As much as Bonnie annoyed me, I'd miss them if they left.

"When did you last see a movie, Aster?" Hattie asked.

"Oh, I don't know. Not since I lived with the coven." On Fridays, they'd hang a large white sheet on the exterior wall of a house, and we'd all sit on blankets and enjoy the performances of long-dead actors. People who never anticipated what the world would become.

"You never talk about the coven," Hattie remarked.

"No," I said simply. "I don't."

I didn't miss the silencing look Victor gave her. Bear

liked to describe him as a fart—silent but deadly. Victor didn't seem to mind the comparison.

Cheers reverberated throughout the village as we walked along the main thoroughfare. The buildings had been styled after a Bavarian village, albeit mainly in black, white, and brown. Once upon a time, buildings came in more colors, but there was no point when you couldn't see them in perpetual darkness. Despite repeated requests to Lord Doran, the villages weren't as well lit as some of the cities and more populated areas.

"Vienna!" a voice cried. A child darted forward to intercept the goat.

"Thank the gods," Bear muttered. "Off you go, Vienna." He smacked the goat's butt.

I dropped the sacks in the village square. "Take what's yours and only what's yours," I said at the top of my lungs.

People crowded around us to raid the sacks and shake our hands.

"The price on your head will go up after this," Glenn said. As the owner of the only pub in the village, Glenn Arbor was popular among Berthold residents. He was someone they turned to in times of trouble as well, like when they lost a row of attached homes to a fire two years ago. Glenn was the one to organize the restoration process and arrange for temporary housing for those misplaced. It was more than Lord Doran would ever do.

"As long as nobody's willing to claim the reward, I don't care if the bounty's a million dollars," I said.

He gave an adamant shake of his head. "Never, Miss Aster. The people here are grateful for you." He angled his head toward the pub. "Can I offer you a pint?"

"What about me?" Bear asked. "I helped."

Glenn clapped him on the back. "Half price. How does that sound?"

Bear shot me a baleful look as we headed toward the pub.

The Dancing Dragon was the heart of Berthold. Glenn ran the establishment along with his wife, Rita, and their twin teenagers, Marcus and Meredith.

Rita was wiping down tables as we entered. She broke into a broad smile at the sight of us. "Our hero returns."

"Heroes," Bear said, but no one seemed to hear him.

"I have a wonderful fidget pie if you're interested," Rita said. "Fresh from the oven, or at least I think it is. I'll have to check with Meredith."

Bear rubbed his stomach. "Sounds perfect."

Hattie raised her hand. "I like fidget pie."

"I like crust," Victor's deep voice rumbled.

I smiled at Rita. "One fidget pie, please."

Bear frowned. "Then what will the rest of you be having?"

Marcus popped up from behind the counter. "Did you kill them?"

"No," I said. "And we left the tax collector on two legs so he could tell Lord Doran what happened."

Marcus's brow furrowed. "If you have to send a message, wouldn't killing him and delivering his head on a spike send a stronger one?"

I slid onto a stool at the counter. "Now you sound like Bonnie."

"Did you know people didn't even realize vampires existed before the Great Eruption? Everybody thought they were fictional."

"Lucky them," I said.

When ten of the world's supervolcanoes erupted simultaneously, Mother Earth spilled the secrets she'd been keeping, including the existence of supernatural beings like vampires, witches, and werewolves. Monsters crawled from the planet's core and spread like a fungus across the globe. The ash and debris from the massive eruptions blocked the sun, allowing vampires to emerge from the shadows and seize control. In a short span of time, humans went from the top of the food chain to food. Anyone with magic became a target for vampires to enslave, employ, or oppress. If it weren't for magic, though, the earth and all its living creatures would've died a long time ago. The vampires recognized the inherent power of those with magic and, as a result, worked tirelessly to control them. My coven was only one example of what happened when the oppressed attempted to revolt. Those were memories best left undisturbed.

"Can't imagine a world without vampires," Bear said, slurping his beer, "although I do try."

"It's good to have goals," Glenn said with a smile.

I drank and let the liquid warm my insides. The Wild was cooler than most places on the planet, and my body seemed to know it. I was always trying to keep warm, which is how the golden cloak became a staple of my wardrobe. The cloak had belonged to my grandmother, and I'd inherited it when my frame was still too small to fill it. Now I considered it a second skin.

"Doran's rangers should be here shortly. Make sure everybody's prepared." I'd calculated the time it would take the tax collector to reach Klondike, as well as the time it would take Doran to organize a new team of rangers to search for us.

Glenn nodded solemnly. "I've already hidden ours. As

far as we're concerned, the tax collector took our payment, and we haven't seen it since."

"Thank you for all you do," Rita said. "I wish there was more we could do to support your efforts."

"You don't turn us in," I replied. "That's gratitude enough."

As we left the pub, I pulled up my cloak to shield my face. I enjoyed hearing the rumors about me. Some claimed I was a man faking a woman's voice. Others said I was a vampire who'd turned on her own kind. Thankfully, nobody who knew the truth said I was Aster Goodfellow, granddaughter of Maya Goodfellow. Twenty years ago, my grandmother had been responsible for an uprising against Lord Doran, now called Hecate's Revolt, and her name was well known to the authorities. Under her leadership, an angry mob stormed Klondike. She'd hoped to replace the vampire with a council and then appeal to House Nilsson to give us our independence. The Wild was cut off from the rest of House territory by calderas. It made no sense to remain under their control. The whole reason Lord Doran had carte blanche here was because nobody could easily access The Wild from the mainland, not that they'd want to anyway. For a civilized area, this territory was more dangerous than most. The Wild and the Outer Territories were only one step up from South America. We were equipped to fight monsters, though, including the one that ruled over us with an iron fist.

The witches and wizards among the rebels had unleashed their magic on the unsuspecting vampires. Still, the revolution was unsuccessful. Unbeknownst to them, Lord Doran had discovered the plan and hired a team of witches from Juneau to protect the vampire officials. My grandmother escaped, but her day of reckoning was still to come.

Maya Goodfellow died during an incident now known as 'the purge'— retribution for the revolt. Doran's rangers had swarmed the coven, killing half the members and burning down our homes. The coven was forced to disband, and the members dispersed.

I lost everything I had left that day. I'd been fighting my own battle ever since.

As we crossed the village square, we were intercepted by a stout woman with brown hair. Her nose and cheeks were dusted with flour. Although I recognized her, I didn't know her name.

"Miss Aster, thank goodness you're here," she said. "Can you come?"

My gaze darted to the road. Any moment now Lord Doran's rangers would come marching into the village.

"We'd be happy to, *Lucinda*," Bear said, giving me a pointed look. He knew me too well.

"Yes, of course," I told her. "Show us the way."

"I'll wait here," Victor said. "Keep a lookout."

The stench hit my nostrils the moment she opened the front door. Instinctively, I lifted my arm to cover my nose.

"I think I'll wait outside," Hattie said, coughing.

Lucinda offered an apologetic look. "Sorry about that. The smell is the least of my concerns at the moment."

We entered the modest house, and Lucinda opened the bedroom door. Bear and I coughed in unison. The room reeked of death.

"What happened? An injury?" I approached the man's bedside with caution.

"No, Xavier came home from work yesterday feeling off. Said he had a fever. By the time he finished his supper, he could barely move from his muscles aching so bad. Now he's oozing from all his pores."

I glanced at the man's sheet-covered body. "Oozing what?"

Bear cringed. "Do we really need to know the details?"

I ignored his squeamishness. "Can you describe the ooze?"

Lucinda pulled back the sheet to reveal a pattern of green and putrid pus. "I'll be scrubbing sheets, towels, and clothes for the rest of my life to get rid of the stench. It's overpowering."

"I've never seen symptoms like this," I said.

"Me neither. Has a healer been to see him?" Bear asked.

Lucinda blew a raspberry. "Frank would have to stay sober long enough to do anything more than drool on him."

Oh, boy. That didn't sound encouraging.

"Has he traveled anywhere recently?" I asked.

"No, just been a normal week for us. Xavier worked over in Whitehead—he's a cobbler there, kids are at school, and I'm rolling dough like always."

"No one else has fallen ill?" I asked.

"Not in our house. Can't speak for anywhere else."

"Has he spoken at all?" Bear asked.

"Nothing I can understand. Fever dreams is my guess." She wrung her hands. "If he dies, I don't know how we'll survive. My bread only brings in so much money, certainly not enough to live on."

I gave her arm a reassuring squeeze. "One day at a time, Lucinda. Let's worry about tomorrow when tomorrow comes."

Her face paled. "Gods above, tomorrow."

Bear and I exchanged looks. "What's tomorrow?" I asked.

"The lottery. Xavier's been chosen." Her hand flew to cover her mouth as she gazed at her sickly husband. "He can't go in this condition."

"Mama." A boy of about seven or eight ran into the room.

"Russell, I told you to go to school with your sister," his mother scolded him. "Your father isn't well, and we don't need you underfoot."

"I only came in to say that you don't need to worry. I can go in papa's place." The little boy puffed out his skinny chest.

Lucinda ushered everyone out of the bedroom and closed the door behind us.

"You know you can't do that." She flashed an apologetic look at us. "Russell's anemic. He'll never be able to donate blood."

The boy tugged her sleeve. "You can't go, mama. Who'll take care of us?"

Lucinda paled. "Your sister can manage."

Russell's eyes brimmed with tears. "What if Daddy dies and you're not here?"

I buckled under the stress of the situation. "I'll go in your husband's place."

The little boy stared at me in wonder. "You would go for my dad?'

"You're right. Your mom can't leave your dad while he's so ill." And I'd be damned if I let them take blood from the other child. I knew they were protected in other parts of the world, but The Wild was—wild.

"I heard they've got fake blood in House August territory," Lucinda said. "All the vampires are drinking it there. I wish it would make its way here."

19

"Even if House Nilsson adopted it, I doubt Lord Doran would follow suit," I said.

Lucinda peered at me. "Are you sure you want to...?"

I placed a hand on her shoulder. "Leave it to me. In the meantime, I think you should ask a healer from one of the neighboring villages to come. I can recommend Mauve Kaminsky. She's in Whitehead."

"I'd also suggest keeping the bedroom door closed and keep your visits to a minimum in case your husband is contagious," Bear added. "You don't want to find yourselves covered in green pus."

"I've been washing my hands constantly." Lucinda held up two hands with cracked skin. "Can't risk contaminating my dough."

"What's going on with the healer, do you think?" Bear asked as we left the house.

"Not sure." Sometimes people cracked under pressure. Or simply gave up.

"Did that lady have a rotting vampire in her oven or something?" Hattie asked, falling in step with us.

"Her husband is sick, and I don't think he's going to make it," I said.

"Is that the reason you offered to do that?" Bear asked.

"Do what?" Hattie asked.

"Swap places with Xavier for the lottery," Bear answered for me.

Hattie smacked my arm. "You did what? Are you insane?"

I kept my gaze fixed on the path ahead. "You heard her, Bear. They're in dire straits."

"You're a wanted witch, Aster," Hattie said. "You can't go waltzing into the belly of the beast and offer up a vein."

"They don't know who I am."

"They'll figure it out real fast when they see glitter in your blood," Hattie said.

I gave her a long look. "There's no glitter in my blood. Besides, I don't actually intend to give any. As long as they get their name ticked off, that's all that matters."

"And how do you propose to make that happen without actually donating blood?" Bear asked.

"I'll figure it out before I get there."

He laughed. "I sure hope so."

A shrill whistle drew our attention to another path. Victor stood at the edge of the village, waving his arms. We hurried to meet him.

"We need to go home this way," he said. "There are rangers headed this way from the main road."

We ducked into the woods and followed a path of our own creation until we arrived at an alternate route to the hideout.

"Have you ever seen anything so putrid in your life?" Bear asked, and proceeded to tell Victor about poor Xavier Joyce. "I'm surprised the odor didn't kill anyone who smelled it. It was more potent than Tyson's body odor."

"You shouldn't joke about it," Hattie said. "That poor woman is about to lose the breadwinner in their family. His death may be quick, but the rest of the family's will be slow and painful." Her gaze dropped to the ground. "This is why bringing a child into this world such a terrible idea."

"What do you think he has?" Victor asked.

I shook my head. "No idea, but it looks like a terrible way to die."

"Maybe it's the work of a vile demon," Hattie suggested.

Victor grunted. "Is there any other kind?"

The forest grew dense as we progressed toward our hideout. A cold wind blew past us, taking me by surprise.

The sudden dip in temperature felt unnatural. Suddenly, the hair on the back of my neck stood on end.

"I think we need to pick up the pace," I said.

Hattie shot me a quizzical glance. "Rangers?"

I quickened my steps. "Something else."

Bear halted in his tracks and turned around to give the area a sweeping glance. "We're nearing the stone benches. Maybe it's our crew hiding."

It wasn't. My gut told me it was something much, much worse.

A scream pierced the air, and icicles shot through my veins.

Beside me, Hattie stiffened. "Who was that?"

Victor craned his neck to look over his shoulder. "The better question is, what was that?"

It didn't take long to find out. A gust of wind nearly knocked me off my feet. I managed to maintain my balance and withdrew an arrow from my quiver, preparing for a fight. Another blast of air jerked the arrow to the left.

"Magic?" Bear asked, casting a quick glance at me.

"I don't think so," I said quietly. Part of me wished it was magic because the alternative seemed much worse.

Maybe it was because he was the largest in our party, or maybe it was because he was nearest when they decided to attack. Either way, Victor had the misfortune of being the chosen target.

An invisible force slammed into the werewolf. He crashed to the ground and immediately sprouted fur. I backed away and tried to locate the source of the attack.

A growl erupted from Victor, and he crouched on all fours without fully shifting, scenting the air for his opponent's location.

"Vampire?" Hattie whispered.

I shook my head. Some vampires could turn invisible, but they didn't fight like this, and one certainly wouldn't attack us alone.

The air crackled with taunting laughter. Finally, she showed herself. Her face was almost translucent, and her eyes burned red. Her white curls were wild and untamed. She wore a white duster over a gauzy white jumpsuit and white leather boots.

"I'm sensing a theme," Bear whispered.

The demon pinned her fiery gaze on Victor. "I challenge you," she said, sounding almost gleeful at the prospect.

"Challenge me to what, exactly?" he snarled.

"If you win, you may ask me for anything you please."

"Anything?" His gaze flicked to us, as though we might suggest a few options.

Hattie shrugged. "World peace?"

"Sunlight would be nice," Bear said. "Can you make that happen?"

The demon's eyes rolled. "If I had a dime for every time someone said sunlight. I'm afraid my powers don't extend that far into time and space."

"You said anything," Victor said in an accusatory tone.

The demon's shoulders slumped. "Shall I provide you with a list of previously approved requests?" She straightened and glared at her opponent. "Oh, that's right. There isn't one—because I always win."

Victor examined her closely. "What happens if you win?"

"If," she repeated and laughed. "The optimism of a white, burly male will never cease to entertain me." Her smile evaporated. "You die, of course."

"Is this your physical form?" Victor asked. "Can I make contact with you?"

There was something horribly wicked about her smile. "You can try."

Victor didn't hesitate. With his head down, he attacked her like a battering ram. The demon sank her clawed hands into his fur and unleashed a primal scream. Hattie and Bear covered their ears.

"Shift, you idiot!" Bear yelled.

"I'm trying," came Victor's muffled reply.

The demon withdrew her claws and tipped Victor's chin up to look at his face. "A handsome specimen, aren't you?"

He made a half-hearted attempt to grab her by the throat, but his hands sliced through the air and crashed into each other.

"Let me touch you," he cried.

Laughing, her translucent body regained its solidity.

I strung my bow and took aim at the demon.

She noticed me and clucked her tongue. "This is between us now, dear heart. The deal has been made. No interference allowed from the peanut gallery."

"Victor, you don't have to do this," Hattie cried.

"Oh, but he does," the demon said. "I am Corentine. Has my reputation not preceded me?"

Bear and I exchanged glances. I wasn't sure whether Corentine was her name or her species. Either way, I was unfamiliar with her. That meant the only way I could assess her strengths and weaknesses was by watching the current fight. It was difficult to watch Victor in a vulnerable position. He had always been one of the strongest of our crew.

Bear advanced toward her, ignoring her declaration. The demon swung an arm wide, and he flew backward, his head slamming against a tree. She kept him pinned there without touching him.

"Don't you listen? There are rules! No one from this realm can interfere! Try again, and you'll be deemed my next opponent."

I lowered my arrow.

"I need to touch you, please," Victor said. He began tearing at his fur with his own claws. "I can't stand the way I feel without you."

"What's she doing to him?" Hattie whispered.

The demon remained incorporeal. "I was willing to allow it, but then you tried to choke me. Is that how we treat each other, dearest?"

Victor gazed at her with love in his eyes. "Never. I would never hurt you. You're a dream come true. A goddess among mortals."

Bear tried to tear himself away from the tree trunk but to no avail.

"Should we do something?" Hattie whispered.

"Listen and learn," the demon replied without looking at us.

I realized I couldn't move. The demon had somehow rendered my feet and arms immobile.

Victor's fur and claws retracted, and he rose to his human height. "I don't want to win a favor by besting you. The only thing I want in this world is to touch you. You get what you want, and I get what I want."

"Very well then. Down, boy," she ordered.

Victor dropped to his knees and fixed the demon with a pleading look. "Take me, Corentine. I'm yours."

Another blast of air forced Victor all the way to the ground. I watched helplessly as the demon covered his darker body with her own white one. With her head at the opposite end, their shape formed the yin and yang symbol. With a final wail, they both disappeared. The wind died, and we were released from our temporary prisons.

I stared at the empty spot on the ground.

"Why did he act like that?" Hattie asked.

Bear's face hardened. "Because the demon did something to him. She fights dirty."

"We need to find out everything we can about this demon and destroy her," Hattie said in a voice that meant business.

"How do you fight a creature like that?" I asked. Mind games and translucence. I'd rather fight Lord Doran than Corentine.

Bear knelt down and scooped a handful of dirt. "RIP, buddy," he said softly, and let the dirt sift through his fingers.

Reluctantly, we dragged ourselves away. I wasn't looking forward to explaining his demise to the rest of the crew. I tugged my cloak around my shoulders and we headed for home.

Chapter Three

The crew held a short memorial for Victor around the campfire. We each shared a story about the quiet werewolf and drank a beer in his honor. I hated that we couldn't do more.

"You okay, Aster?" Scarlet asked as I collected the empty glasses.

"Feels like my fault."

"How? You didn't summon the demon."

"He was a member of my crew. If I hadn't ordered us to return the sacks, he wouldn't have crossed Corentine's path."

"I think that's a reach," Scarlet said. "Victor knew what he signed up for. He was glad to be one of us."

I didn't tell her about our encounter with the Joyce family. I figured I'd get home from the donation center tomorrow and then tell everyone what I'd done. Thankfully, Bear and Hattie seemed to forget everything that happened prior to Victor's death.

I climbed to the tree house and attempted to sleep. I sprawled across the mattress and focused on the wooden beams that formed my ceiling. Even in absolute darkness, I knew every crack. Every crevice. I replayed the encounter with Corentine in my mind fifty times, each time trying to come up with a better outcome. I could've used my magic, but that would've alerted the rangers to our location. Or maybe the demon's invisible hand would've prevented me from using magic. I couldn't be sure.

I rolled on my side and groaned. Every day, there was some new threat. A new challenge. My dream was to live in a place without constant strife, where my choices weren't taken from me by those in positions of power. Where I could be myself and revel in my magic rather than hide it.

But that was not the world we lived in.

Despite the absence of sunrise and sunset, our bodies seemed to know when to sleep and when to wake. The cities tended to simulate night and day to the best of their ability, whereas The Wild and its villages were more prone to follow their own schedule. I knew I hadn't slept a full eight hours, not even close. Then again, I probably hadn't slept eight hours in a row since I was a child.

I grabbed a spare cloak, leaving my golden one behind, and crept out of the hideout before anyone saw me. I knew I shouldn't have offered to take Xavier Joyce's place, but their situation seemed so hopeless. If Lucinda showed up for the lottery today, there was every chance she wouldn't be with her family when her husband died. I would want someone to do the same for me if I were in her shoes.

I reached into my pocket and curled my fingers around the coins for reassurance. Minor officials in The Wild are as corrupt as they come. I'd have to choose my target carefully, of course, but I felt confident I could persuade them to overlook me. I had no choice. If I let them take my blood, I'd give them a new reason to pursue me. I wasn't an ordinary witch, not like June with her water magic or Patricia with her fire magic. My grandmother had been a coven leader from a powerful family, and some of that power had trickled down to me. My grandmother saw it in me from an early age, even before I showed any sign of talent. Although not a seer, she seemed to have a sixth sense about things. I once asked her why she stayed in The Wild if she suspected how bad things would become. She told me the only way out of it was through it. I didn't understand then. To be fair, I wasn't sure I understood now. Her rebellion had failed, resulting in the purge, and we were still squirming under Doran's iron fist.

I arrived at Klondike, the official headquarters of House Nilsson in The Wild. The donation center was located here, as well as Lord Doran's office and residence. Although the vampire had places in Anchorage and Juneau, too, he was rarely away from The Wild. According to local gossip, King Stefan had appointed him as thegn and given him the title 'Lord Doran' in return for service during battles that secured land for House Nilsson. There was one vampire between them in rank—Lord John Birney, Earl of the Outer Territories. My grandmother had explained that House Nilsson had adopted a hybrid peerage system, mixing Anglo Saxon with the more modern British system. Lord Birney spent his time traveling throughout the Outer Territories, so we only had to contend with Lord Doran most of the time, which was more than enough.

I entered the donation center and took a seat in the sterile waiting area. Everything was white, from the floor to the walls to the furniture. It looked like a clinic in outer space.

"Shouldn't there be thirty of us?" the young man beside me asked. "I only count twenty-two."

"Is that unusual?" I asked.

"It means we'll have to give more to make up for those missing." He folded his arms and slumped against the chair. "Nice team effort."

I thought of Xavier Joyce and wondered whether other families had been hit by a mysterious illness. Other families that didn't happen to have a visitor with a savior complex.

"My neighbor's supposed to be here, too, but he's real sick," an older woman across from us said. "I tried to check on him but couldn't make it past the door. The smell was nauseating."

My head snapped to attention. "Does he live alone?"

She nodded. "That's why I decided to knock for him. Thought we could ride over together. I called his name, but he didn't answer."

"You didn't send for help?" the young man asked. His judgmental tone didn't escape me.

The woman shrugged. "Help from where? With what money? Last I checked, healers don't work for free."

"Ashby," a vampire called.

The older woman rose to her feet, bones creaking. "This'll be my last year. I age out after this, thank the gods. I'm like a walking pin cushion."

"Excuse me," I said. "What's the name of your neighbor? I might know someone who can check on him."

"Wilton," she said as she passed by. "Devon Wilton. We live in Whitehead."

She disappeared behind the white curtain.

The young man looked at me. "You'd send someone to a stranger's house?"

"Do you live alone?"

He nodded. "Used to live with my dad, but he passed two years ago."

"Wouldn't you want someone to check on you if you were violently ill?"

He didn't answer. Instead, he said, "You don't have any marks."

I realized he was referring to my arms. I tugged down the sleeves of my cloak. "I heal easily," I said, which wasn't completely untrue. My grandmother told me my grandfather had been a wizard with healing magic, which he'd passed down to me. Although I couldn't heal anybody else, my own injuries seemed to resolve more quickly than they should.

"Wish I healed fast." He held out his right arm to show me the evidence of his previous donations. "They'll have to do the left today, but the veins are crap on that side." He patted his pocket. "At least I've got my painkillers ready for afterward."

A vampire behind the counter consulted the list in his hand. "Joyce," he said, scanning the room.

I shot up from my chair and raised my hand. "Here I am."

"You're Xavier Joyce?"

"His wife." I strode toward him, giving my best impression of someone happy to donate to our vampire overlords. "What's your name? I haven't seen you here before," I said in a friendly manner.

The vampire's gaze raked over me. "Don't think I've seen you either. Would've remembered such a pretty hair color."

I palmed two coins and offered my hand. "Lucinda Joyce."

He took my hand, and I let the coins go. His expression didn't change. "Garrison, although we don't usually introduce ourselves to the donors, you know."

"Oh, I know, but I like to make an impression."

A grin tugged at the corners of his mouth. "I'll bet." He slid his hand into his pocket and deposited the coins.

"Does this have to be so clinical?" I asked, waving a hand airily. "I'm sure there's a way to make this more enjoyable for everyone involved."

His fangs poked his lower lip. "Now you're speaking my language."

"There's a feedback box on your way out," the vampire next to him said without looking up from her paperwork. "You can fill out a comment card and leave it there."

"Perfect."

"Come on back," Garrison said.

"It's my turn," his co-worker said.

"You get the next one."

For a moment, I thought my scheme might not work. My heart pounded as we stepped into a vestibule, and he pulled the white curtain across. He pointed to the chair, and I sat, weighing my options. I had to get out of here without a fight.

Relief rippled through me when the vampire put a finger to his lips. "You've got good veins," he said, a touch louder than necessary.

"That's what everyone tells me," I replied.

He didn't move. Another minute later, he drew the curtain aside and ushered me out.

"She's done," Garrison said, as we arrived at the counter.

"Is she?" his companion queried.

Garrison adopted a firmer tone. "I said she's done. Mark her off."

His companion wrote a checkmark next to the Joyce name.

I winked at Garrison. "See you next time."

He couldn't stop grinning at me. "Looking forward to it."

"Stop right there," a security guard called as I tried to exit.

I kept walking, feigning ignorance.

"I said stop!"

The entrance door swung open and in stepped a tall, dark-haired vampire with chiseled features and deep-set hazel eyes.

I narrowly avoided a collision.

The security guard bowed. "I'm sorry, Lord Doran. I tried to clear a path, but some people don't know how to listen." The guard glared at me.

"Never mind." Doran's gaze landed on me and our eyes locked. I'd never seen him up close before. He seemed larger at this distance, broader and well defined. His irises were rimmed with golden flecks that reminded me of my magic. Oh, the irony.

I broke eye contact and pressed my back against the wall to give him room to pass. His gaze lingered on me for another moment before he continued into the donation center.

"Lord Doran," I heard Garrison say. "We weren't expecting you until tomorrow."

I slipped outside and released the breath I'd been holding. Rangers filed past me. Nobody gave me a backward glance. I'd heard the vampire made visits to the donation center, as well as other royal establishments, but had never seen it in practice. I was relieved I'd gotten Xavier ticked off the list before the vampire's arrival.

I returned to the hideout to pick up a few supplies before heading to Whitehead. The entire crew was assembled around the campfire. Bonnie nudged Scarlet's leg when she saw me.

"Where were you?" Scarlet asked.

"An errand."

"I didn't realize your errands now include blood donations."

I looked at Hattie, who lowered her gaze to the ground.

"It's fine. Crisis averted."

Bear held out a mug for me.

"Thanks." I cradled it in my hands and inhaled the aroma of peppermint tea.

"How did you manage to avert this particular crisis?" Bonnie asked.

"I bribed a donations officer." I sipped the tea, grateful for the extra warmth.

"You only bought that family time, you know," Bonnie said.

I peered at her over the top of my mug. "And? What's your point?"

Bonnie averted her gaze. "Forget it."

"There's another man who's sick," I told them. "I'm heading to Whitehead as soon as I've eaten something."

"Same cheerful green sores?" Bear asked.

"Sounds like it."

He cringed. "I'll sit this one out."

Scarlet insisted on joining me.

"I don't think you want to do that," Hattie warned.

"I have a strong constitution. I'll be fine."

"It may not be the same affliction as Xavier," I said, "but I feel like we should check on him either way."

"Why not send a healer to check on him?" Bear asked. "Why subject yourself to it?"

"Because she's a control freak," Bonnie interrupted.

"Why let someone do their job when Aster can do it for you?"

I clenched my jaw but said nothing.

"Come on, Aster. Hurry up and eat. Whitehead is a hike." Scarlet slung a bag over her shoulder.

"You can take the Beast," Tyson offered.

"Safer not to," I told him. Rangers would still be on the hunt for the vehicle. Best not to dangle it in front of their faces.

Bear passed me a parcel of cheese and bread. I ate hungrily between sips of tea.

"You'll have to start saving your extras for me if I get pregnant," Bonnie told him.

He looked at her askance. "That wasn't extra. That was Aster's portion."

Bonnie appeared unconvinced.

I gobbled it down, including every crumb of bread I picked off my cloak. "Anyone else aside from Scarlet?"

Everybody mumbled at once. I heard "chores" and "too tired."

I retrieved my longbow from weapons storage.

"Are you planning to shoot him if he isn't already dead?" Hugo asked.

I feigned a laugh. "Very funny."

Although if Devon Wilton's condition was even half as bad as Xavier Joyce's, I couldn't rule out the possibility.

Chapter Four

S carlet and I traveled on foot to the village of Whitehead. It was hard not to think about Victor as a breeze swirled the hem of my cloak around my ankles.

"You okay?" Scarlet asked.

"Thinking about Victor. Spent most of my sleeping hours wondering if there was more I could've done."

"Sounds like the demon had strange abilities. Hattie was ranting about her while you were gone."

"Maybe it'll be good if Hattie obsesses. We need someone to do the research so we can fight the demon if she dares to show her face again."

Scarlet glanced at my arm. "I'm glad you were able to avoid getting blood drawn."

"I wasn't too worried."

She snickered. "We should all have your attitude."

"Lord Doran was there."

Scarlet blew out a breath. "Wow. The thegn himself. Why?"

"Seemed like a standard visit."

"Did he notice you?" she asked.

"Not really. I almost stepped on his toes, but I managed to get out of the way in time."

"Moments like that is when concealing your identity comes in handy."

I nodded. "Didn't have my cloak on either." I only tended to wear the golden cloak during the course of what I deemed 'official business,' which mainly included being a thorn in the side of vampires.

The village of Whitehead came into view. It didn't share Berthold's Bavarian charm. Instead, it was more rustic, with log cabins and other structures made primarily of wood. The square was smaller, and the buildings were generally shorter in stature.

I stopped at a food cart and addressed the proprietor. "Can you point us in the direction of Devon Wilton's house?"

He gestured behind us. "Straight down Sleigh Bell Lane. First house on the left."

"Thank you."

"Heard the cobbler died."

The news didn't surprise me.

Scarlet lingered to ogle the sandwiches, but I couldn't think about food at this point. Not when I might encounter that same foul odor.

By the time I reached the house, Scarlet had caught up with me. She held half a sandwich in one hand and the rest dangled from her mouth.

"I won't even ask what kind," I said. She and I didn't share the same preferences. I blamed the wolf in her.

"You sure about this?" Scarlet asked, swallowing the bite she'd taken. "Bear said the other house smelled like rotting corpses."

"There may actually be a rotting corpse inside here." I motioned to the door. "It's locked. Can you get us in?"

Scarlet was an expert at picking locks, among other talents. "Do I look like an amateur to you?"

Placing the other half of her sandwich in her mouth, she removed a hairpin from her hair. Then she bent down and worked the lock until I heard a gentle click. She opened the door and immediately yanked it closed again.

"Rotting corpse smell, huh?"

Scarlet turned and let the sandwich drop from her mouth into her hand. "No way am I going in there."

"Are you sure it's the smell that made you want to vomit? Maybe you're pregnant."

She craned her neck to glare at me. "My name isn't Bonnie. I'm not looking to get knocked up."

"She and Bear seem very happy."

"Whatever. Bonnie just wants someone to take care of her for life. She figures if she has Bear's kid, he'll feel beholden."

"He loves her."

"He loves the idea of a little Bear running around. He's kidding himself if he thinks that's possible for any of us. We're outlaws."

"Quite the skeptic, you are."

"I prefer realist. Anyway, you know there won't be any little Scarlets running around unless I request one of the guys as a sperm donor."

"Put a blond wig on Tyson and pretend he's Bonnie."

Scarlet grimaced. "Now I'm really going to lose my lunch. Bonnie's not remotely my type."

"I thought you liked blondes."

"Yeah, but I don't like bitches."

I opened the door. "Wait here."

"You don't have to tell me twice. I'm going to forget I ever smelled that so I can enjoy the rest of my sandwich."

I inched inside the cabin and tried not to breathe through my nose. Flies had already gathered on dirty plates in the kitchen.

"Mr. Wilton," I called. "My name is Aster. I've come to check on you. Your neighbor said you aren't doing well." I stopped outside the bedroom door. It stood ajar, so I nudged it open with the toe of my boot. "Mr. Wilton?"

The figure on the bed was perfectly still. I crept forward, holding my cloak in front of my nose and mouth. Flies buzzed around the room and I swatted them away.

"You poor bastard," I whispered.

Like Xavier, Devon Wilton's skin was covered in green sores. Also like Xavier, Devon Wilton was dead.

I decided not to linger. I had no clue whether this lethal illness was contagious and didn't want to risk increased exposure.

"That bad?" Scarlet asked, as I closed the front door behind me and gasped for breath.

"He's dead."

"Same pretty green hue?"

I nodded. "We need to report this and then find out if anyone else is sick."

"Did those guys know each other? They don't even live in the same village."

"No, but Xavier worked in Whitehead. Maybe they worked together or shared a meal."

Scarlet drank from her water pouch. "Gee, that narrows it down. We'll just knock on every door and see whether anybody saw them together this week."

I started walking back toward the center of the village. "We can start with anywhere that serves food."

"Suits me. I can eat again."

I shot her a pointed look. "We're trying to determine whether the food is contaminated."

Her face fell. "Right. No food then." She clutched her stomach. "Why did you let me eat that sandwich?"

"You were too fast." I motioned to the village square. "Why don't you question the food cart guy while I report the death." Then I'd check with other food establishments.

"On it. And if he didn't serve them, I may get another sandwich for the walk home. Investigations give me an appetite."

"Breathing gives you an appetite."

We separated when we reached the square. I turned left and went straight to the village clerk's office. There was no line, which was good. I didn't want to be overheard and incite mass panic.

"Can I help you?" the clerk asked. The name plate on the counter identified him as Larry Gale.

"Devon Wilton is dead. I'd suggest whoever removes the body wears a mask and gloves."

He frowned. "You think it can be contracted through the air?"

"At this point, I don't know, but I'd recommend taking precautions until we know more. This is the second case this week."

Larry blinked in surprise. "Who else died?"

"Someone in Berthold."

"And the cause of death?"

"An illness I haven't seen before." I described the symptoms.

Larry's eyes widened more with each new detail. "That sounds awful."

"The smell is the worst part." From my point of view, anyway. Devon probably had a different opinion.

Larry eyed me closely. "Can I ask your name?"

"Concerned citizen." I turned and left before he could ask any more questions. The only information he needed to gather was from Devon Wilton's house.

I walked past a row of shops until I reached the first one that served food.

"Welcome to the Lunar Cafe," a woman said as I entered.

The decor was rustic chic, with metal tables and chairs painted in cheerful colors. Green valances lined the windows, and moody paintings of the phases of the moon adorned the walls.

"Not too busy today," I said.

"We're in between rushes. What can I tempt you with?"

I browsed the options behind the glass, even though I had no intention of eating anything.

"It all looks amazing, but I'm interested in information today."

Her eyebrows inched up. "What kind of information?"

"Do you know Devon Wilton?"

"Sure. He made these." She touched the glasses that sat on the bridge of her nose.

"He was an optician?"

Her face registered surprise. "Was?"

"I'm sorry to tell you that he's dead."

Her expression crumpled. "Oh, that's a shame. He was a nice man. Any idea what happened?"

"He got sick."

"Really? I saw him yesterday morning, and he looked right as rain. He stopped by for a poppyseed muffin on his way to work."

41

"Where's his office?"

She angled her head. "The outskirts of the village. There's a section with service providers. Glasses. Seamstress. That sort of thing."

"Do you also know Xavier Joyce?"

She shook her head. "Should I?"

"He lived in Berthold, but he was a cobbler here."

"I mend my own shoes, so I didn't know him." Her brow creased. "He's dead, too? What kind of sickness is this?"

"One that has a putrid odor. I'm still nauseated."

She offered a sympathetic smile. "I'd offer you ginger for the nausea, but I'm low on supplies."

"Vampires?"

"I assume so. A few of my herbs out back went missing two weeks ago. At first, I thought it might be woodland critters out for a snack, but there's no sign of chewing. I considered warding the area, but..."

"You didn't want to get caught."

Her mouth formed a thin line. "I'd rather do without than suffer the consequences of illegal magic."

Magic was only permissible under certain circumstances and only under the watchful eye of our vampire overlords.

"If you're right about the vampires, then they won't turn you in unless you block their access." Without her, they'd have to find a new source for supplies.

"That was my thinking. As long as I leave it unwarded, we both get what we want."

"Would you mind if I took a look at your garden?"

She seemed taken aback. "Not at all."

We ventured to the back door, and she held it open for me. "Are you looking for something in particular?"

"I'll know it when I see it." Maybe.

"You're that Goodfellow girl, aren't you? Aster. The one who antagonizes Lord Doran's rangers. I'd recognize that shade of red anywhere." She motioned to my hair.

"It's auburn."

"Well, your grandmother's hair was a brilliant red, like an angry flame I used to say. Hot and eager to burn."

I smiled. "Sounds about right."

"I'm Ingrid, by the way. You probably don't remember me."

"Were you a member of our coven?"

She nodded. "I was always in the greenhouse with dirty hands." Holding up her hands, she wiggled her fingers. "Earth witch."

"I thought I knew everybody who stayed in The Wild after the purge."

"Some of us sort of melted away, trying our best to forget the past. I moved here and opened this place. Mainly keep to myself, except for serving customers."

I examined a couple potted plants and read the labels. "You use these as ingredients in your food?"

"Yes, indeed. I tend to choose plants that I can grow in shade, but a few require encouragement."

"Which ones are missing?"

She pointed to empty spots. "Ginger and anemone nemorosa."

I gave her a blank look.

"Windflower?" she prompted.

"Sorry, my education got cut short."

Ingrid offered a sympathetic smile. "You're not the only one. I do so little magic these days that I find myself forgetting the basics sometimes." She shook her head in dismay. "I'm embarrassed for myself."

"Are these the types of plants you grew for the coven?" I

remembered the greenhouse itself, but none of the details. I didn't even recall seeing the inside, although I must have.

"Some, but not all. My earth magic leaned toward food provisions rather than remedies. There were other witches who specialized in the healing arts."

"Like Mauve."

Ingrid didn't smile at the mention of the healer. "Yes, like Mauve."

I opted not to pry. I had other priorities at the moment. "Do you think these plants were chosen at random?"

"Hard to say. If a sickness is making the rounds, maybe somebody wanted to avoid paying a healer and tried to help themselves."

"I can understand ginger, but why the other one?"

"Windflower has healing properties, although I doubt the average person knows that. I sell it to healers. It isn't easy to grow. The soil has to be kept moist."

Maybe Devon had been the one to steal them when he first experienced symptoms, although Ingrid said the theft happened two weeks ago, so it was unlikely.

"Do you happen to know if Devon had a favorite spot to eat?"

She smiled. "Aside from here, you mean? He liked Pike's Peak like every other male in Whitehead."

"What's so great about Pike's Peak?"

"I think they like the servers and tolerate the food."

Got it. "I'll pay them a visit."

"The girls are sweet, but I wouldn't want any daughter of mine to work there. I think they must burn calories just swatting away all the grabby hands."

"You said Devon was a nice guy."

"He was to me. Then again, I'm of the age that men no longer notice me unless I'm giving them something they want, and sometimes not even then." She laughed at her own joke.

"Thanks for your help, Ingrid. I appreciate it."

I left the Lunar Cafe and made my way to Pike's Peak. It was unlikely to be teeming with grabby hands at this hour. Maybe I'd manage to catch a few of the girls during their downtime.

The exterior of the building was plain with only a small sign that indicated the name of the establishment. No wonder I'd never noticed it before.

Music blasted my eardrums the moment I stepped through the entrance. Scantily clad young women served patrons at the bar as well as the dining area. I wasn't sure how they managed to avoid hypothermia. The restaurant wasn't particularly warm.

A hostess sauntered over to me. "Table for one?"

"I'd like to speak to the manager."

Her smile faded. "Got a name?"

"Aster."

"If you're looking for a job, I can tell you right now he won't hire you."

I burst into laughter. "How old do you think I am?"

"Not your age. Your hair. He doesn't like redheads. Thinks they might turn into monsters and eat him."

"Good thing my hair is auburn."

The hostess shrugged. "You say potato." She turned on her heel, expecting me to follow.

Considering the limited number of patrons, the volume of the music seemed excessive. I began to wonder whether the noise was a cover for an illegal gambling ring or something worse.

The hostess delivered me to a closed door. "He's in

here." She banged on the door with her fist. "Evan, you got a visitor!"

"Come in," came the gruff response.

The moment the door closed behind me, there was silence. I looked around the room. No speakers. It took a second for my ears to adjust.

The manager gave me the once-over. His gaze settled on my hair. "You need work?"

"No. I need answers."

Looking visibly relieved, he motioned to the empty chair across from him. "What's your name, sweetheart?"

"Aster Goodfellow," I said, lowering myself into the armchair.

His mouth dropped open. "You're her? The Hooded One?"

"I prefer Aster."

He fell back against his chair and stared at me in wonder. "Wow. I know you make the rounds sometimes, but I've never seen you with my own eyes."

I tapped my fingers on the arms of the chair. "Well, here I am."

"You have no idea the good you've done for this community. Seriously. Amazing stuff."

"Thank you."

"Tell me what I can do for you. Please. I want to give back." His hands didn't seem to stop moving. Every word came with a gesture attached to it.

"Do you know Devon Wilton?"

His brow creased. "Sure. I know all my best customers."

"When was the last time you saw him?"

The manager stroked his chin. "I'd say three days ago. He came in for a meal with his buddy, Emery."

Food eaten three days ago was worth investigating. "Do you remember what Devon ordered?"

"No, but I can find out." He let loose an obnoxious whistle. "Trina!"

A young woman burst into the office and music flooded the room. "What's the emergency?"

"This nice lady would like to know what Devon Wilton ordered last time he was here." His gaze skated to me. "Trina remembers damn near everything. She can tell you what color shirt you wore on a Tuesday three weeks ago."

"Oh, stop. You know it's just my weird brain." Trina's cheeks seemed strained from all that smiling. "Devon had a frittata and a side of roasted potatoes." She appeared thoughtful for a moment. "And one beer. He ordered two, but Emery drank the second one."

"Did he seem normal to you?" I asked.

A high-pitched giggle erupted from Trina. "Define normal."

"Did he seem different than he usually is? Any complaints?"

She shook her head. "No. He seemed the same as always. His only complaint was about a difficult customer who wanted his glasses with one frame green and one frame orange."

"Any idea where I can find Emery?" I asked.

"He works at the post office," Trina said.

"Is he a vampire?" Federal jobs generally were restricted to vampires.

"He works in the sorting room," Trina clarified. "Not at the counter. If you're planning to talk to him now, though, he lives on Colt's Court. His shift at work won't be until later."

The manager grinned at her. "See? She remembers everything."

"Thank you. I appreciate the help."

"What's going on with Devon?" Trina asked. "Is he in some kind of trouble?"

"I'm sorry to say he's dead."

The young woman flinched.

"That's unfortunate," the manager said in a quiet voice. "We'll raise a glass to him later, won't we, Trina?"

Tears shimmered in Trina's eyes. "Everybody dies so young here. I ought to move to the mainland before my number is up."

"I don't know that you'd fare better anywhere else," Evan said.

"Might as well take my chances. I feel like a sitting duck in The Wild." She left the office and closed the door behind her, shutting out the loud music once more.

"What's with the high volume?" I asked.

"We get a lot of customers who are hearing impaired."

"What caused that?"

"Vampires. Some have nerve damage from overzealous fangs. Others got passed a virus that resulted in hearing loss." He regarded me. "It's nothing witches like you have to worry about. Just a consequence of being human in a vampire's world."

I had no idea.

He pumped his fist in the air. "Keep fighting the good fight. It's been an honor to meet you." He gave my hand an aggressive shake.

I left Pike's Peak, pinched with guilt over the manager's revelation. How did I not know a segment of the population suffered from hearing loss? Some hero of the people I was.

I kicked myself all the way to Colt's Court, a quiet

street, except for the children playing street hockey. Two girls and three boys.

"I'm looking for Emery," I told them.

One of the girls pointed to a house at the end of the court. The nondescript building squatted over half an acre of dirt. I was about to knock when the front door opened, and a man emerged. Medium build, he wore a dark green turtleneck sweater and jeans. His thick beard covered most of his face.

"Are you Emery?"

His gaze flicked over me. "I am."

I was no healer, but he looked healthy to me. "I'm afraid I have sad news. Devon Wilton is dead."

Emery's eyes blinked rapidly. "Dead? How'd that happen?"

"He was very ill. I'm trying to figure out what made him so sick."

Emery rubbed his forehead. "This doesn't make any sense. Devon wasn't ill. I saw him yesterday morning coming out of Lunar Cafe. He was fine."

"Well, he contracted something between then and now. He had green sores all over his body. Whatever it was took him down fast."

Emery cringed. "Green sores? He wasn't in a relationship, and he didn't pay for the company of women, if that's what you want to know."

I'd been so focused on food that a sexually transmitted disease hadn't occurred to me. "What about meals? His isn't the only case. I'm trying to determine if both men got sick from the same food."

Emery folded his arms and pondered the question. "It can't be what he ate because my wife cooked it."

"I thought you said the last time you saw him was yesterday morning."

"It was, but my wife dropped off a casserole for him. He was supposed to join us for dinner, but he said he wasn't feeling up to it and went home instead. I assumed he meant mentally. We had plenty, so Maria dropped it on his doorstep. We all ate it, though. Me, Maria, the kids. Nobody's sick."

It seemed Devon wasn't feeling well by dinnertime, which suggested the illness had already taken hold of him by then.

"What about lunch? Any idea what he might've eaten?"

"He usually packs a lunch and eats at his office. I can't say for certain about yesterday, but that'd be my guess." He caught sight of something over my shoulder and yelled, "Rocco, you be nice to your sister, or I'm taking your puck and stick!" He gave me a sheepish grin. "Sorry about that. Kids, you know?"

I envied their semblance of normalcy. My childhood ended abruptly the day of the purge.

"Thanks for your help," I said. "If anybody gets sick, will you let me know? My name is Aster Goodfellow."

He gave me an appraising look. "I know that name. You're the one who steals from vamps and gives us the money."

I placed a finger to my lips. "That's between you and me."

"My wife and I appreciate everything you do. Hey, let me send you home with something to eat. It's the least we can do."

I waved him off. "There's no need, but thank you."

"Where can I find you, Aster?"

"Tell the birds. Word will get to me."

Emery scanned the treetops as though on the hunt for birds. "Everybody says they work for witches. I always assumed it was an old wives' tale."

I smiled. "And who do you think those old wives really were?"

Scarlet waited for me in the village square. I could tell by her posture that something was wrong.

She marched toward me. "What the hell, Aster? I've been looking everywhere for you."

"I thought we were dividing and conquering. What's wrong?"

"I overheard two guys talking. They were on their way to Berthold."

"Is someone else sick?"

"No." Her face grew pinched. "But I think your lottery friend is dead."

Chapter Five

The hideout was quiet when Scarlet and I finally returned. She sprinted to the outhouse to relieve an upset stomach.

"I told you not to eat all those sandwiches," I called after her.

I found Hattie seated with her back against a tree, a book open in her lap.

"Hey, Hattie. What are you reading?"

She looked up at me. "I'm researching the demon that killed Victor."

It hadn't occurred to me how hard Hattie might take his death. It was easy to forget she was younger than the rest of us and hadn't experienced as much death as we had.

I settled beside her under the canopy of the tree. "What did you find out so far?"

"Corentine absorbed his essence. That's what she does."

"Would she really have done whatever he wanted if Victor had won? Does she have that kind of power?"

"According to the book, yes. She's similar to jinn in that way. She basically grants you a wish if you win."

"Well, they're demons, too, so I guess that makes sense." I leaned closer to read over her shoulder. "Does it say how to defeat her?"

Hattie shook her head. "It says she employs different tactics depending on her opponent. She assesses your essence and identifies weaknesses she can exploit."

"So whatever mojo she worked on Victor isn't necessarily what she'd do to you or me."

"Exactly."

I hugged my knees. "Makes it hard to prep for another encounter."

Hattie shuddered. "I hope she's moved on from here."

"Then why bother with the research?"

Hattie turned her solemn eyes to me. "In case she hasn't."

I lifted the book's cover so I could read the title. "Where did you find this?" There were no libraries in The Wild. The nearest one was in Fairbanks and it wasn't very good. Books weren't a priority for Lord Doran. More accurately, the vampires limited our access to books in order to limit our knowledge.

"Olive McMurtry. You know her, right?"

"I do." Olive owned a used bookstore and cafe in Oglethorpe, a village northeast of Whitehead. "You went all the way there by yourself?"

"Tyson went with me, but he made me hurry back because he had to go."

"Go where?"

She shrugged. "Some secret mission too dangerous for me to be a part of. I wish they'd stop treating me like a kid."

My mind was stuck on 'secret mission.' "Did he say where they were going?"

"No. I tried to eavesdrop, but they were all whispering."

I didn't like the sound of that.

She looked at me. "I guess it was a secret from you, too, huh?"

"Guess so." Or maybe they knew I was preoccupied with the investigation and didn't want to burden me. I wanted to give my crew the benefit of the doubt.

I stood upright. "I'm going to see what I can find out."

Her expression turned hopeful. "Can I come?"

"I think you're doing important work here, and you should keep going."

"You're not just saying that?"

"Absolutely not, Hattie. Research is every bit as important as fieldwork. Sometimes you can't do one without the other."

She seemed to accept my response. "I'm sorry I don't know more about where they went."

"That's okay. I can figure it out."

I checked with Scarlet before returning to my tree house. She didn't know anything about this secret mission either. Definitely a red flag.

"I can shift and try to track them," Scarlet said.

"I doubt that'll be easy given the number of times they've been in and out of the hideout this week. I'll climb to the crow's nest and see if I catch a glimpse of them."

"Good idea. Meanwhile, I'll curl into the fetal position and regret my choices."

I climbed up the tree to my house but didn't continue to the crow's nest. Instead, I sat cross-legged on the floor. I tried to limit my use of this particular skill. The more I used it, the more likely I was to get caught, and I didn't want anyone to know.

I closed my eyes and concentrated on my breathing. A deep breath in through my mouth for ten seconds. A slow breath out through my nostrils for eight seconds. It wasn't an exact science, but that was my system. I continued the breathing exercise and focused on separating from my body. My grandmother called it astral projection. She was the only other person in our coven with that ability. She and my parents were the only ones who knew I could do it. They'd tried to hide my light magic, too, but I'd had trouble controlling it and ended up showing my hand, literally.

Astral projection was a great talent to have for reconnaissance purposes. Right now, I intended to use it to find my crew.

The advantage to projecting was that I could float like a ghost and cover terrain more quickly. I guided my incorporeal body above the trees. The higher I floated, the better my view of the whole area. It didn't take me long to spot a cluster of cloaked silhouettes moving together through the darkness. The only place in that direction was Remy's Bog. Why would they be headed there?

I swiveled to see a group of riders on horses coming from Klondike. They seemed to be headed toward the bog, too. What had I missed?

My projection snapped back to my body. The moment I recovered from the transition, I shot to my feet and shimmied to the ground.

"Where are you going?" Scarlet called, as I grabbed my quiver and bow.

"Don't worry. I'll be back!"

"You don't need me?"

"Stay with Hattie. I'll take care of it."

The only way to beat the horses there was to drive. I raced toward the Beast's hiding spot and was relieved to find it still there. I jumped into the 4x4 and sped off.

Because I knew the route the vampires were taking, I

was able to cut a path to the bog where they wouldn't notice my tracks.

I parked the Beast between two dense copses and bolted for the bog. The horses must've been moving faster than I realized because I arrived in time to see them barreling down on my crew.

I strung my bow and took aim at the vampire in the lead. There was no clear shot because of the armor he wore, and I refused to shoot the horse. The rangers started appearing in armor a couple years ago because of the poison-tipped arrows I sometimes used. They must have had a limited supply, though, because not all rangers wore armor, and it wasn't all the time. They only tended to ride horses when they anticipated a run-in with werewolves, knowing the uneasy relationship between horses and wolves.

It was doubtful the vampires knew this was a bog. They tended to keep to major roadways unless they were hunting for something or someone, usually us.

I lowered my bow as I watched the scene unfold. One by one horses collapsed on the ground, felled by an unseen hand. What was happening? No one on my team had yet to move. They remained positioned behind the hill across the bog.

As the horses fell, their riders were dumped into what appeared to be covered pits. They were easy targets now, which my crew must've sensed because they emerged from behind the hill with their weapons drawn. I spotted Hugo with my spare longbow.

Whatever plan they'd concocted, it was working without my involvement. Hugo charged along with the rest of the crew. They must have dug the pits in advance and then lured the vampires to the bog. When did they plan this, and more importantly, why did they hide it from me? Probably because they knew I'd object. Scarlet, too.

Nausea rolled over me as I watched arrow after arrow penetrate the horses' hides. It was a massacre. With the horses sidelined and the vampires stuck in the pits, the wolves tore across the bog and made short work of the riders. I scanned the area for any sign of valuables, any reason for this ploy.

There was nothing.

The sound of vampires crying in pain cut through the other noise. Nobody deserved to suffer like that, not even them. It sickened me.

I stepped closer to the bog. "Get behind the hill," I ordered.

The wolves seemed to notice me for the first time. They slunk away from the bog and sought refuge out of sight.

Hugo marched toward me with his hands balled into fists. "What do you think you're doing?"

"I was going to ask you the same question."

His stare was hard and inscrutable. "Let the crew finish what they started. You can't save them now."

I didn't flinch. "Wasn't planning on it."

It took him a moment to understand. He sneered at the trapped vampires. "Why would you show them mercy?"

I ignored his question. I had too many of my own that required answers. "I don't see any loot. What was the point of this?"

"The point is that vampires are our enemy."

"What about the horses? What justification do you have for killing them?"

"This is war, Aster. That means casualties."

"We aren't at war," I said softly. "This isn't even a battle. This was an unprovoked massacre. And how dare you use my arrows for such a purpose. I would never have consented, and you know it."

Hugo's mouth tightened like the string of my bow. "The last I checked, you're a figurehead in name only. That doesn't give you the right to call each and every shot. This was my plan, and I executed it flawlessly, until you showed up."

"Trust me, I'm doing you a favor." My magic would get rid of the evidence, as well as stop the vampires from suffering. I'd call it a win-win, except there were no winners today.

Red-faced, Hugo lingered for another moment before deciding to obey. He disappeared behind the hill with the wolves and they shielded their faces.

I stood at the edge of the bog and raised my palms in the air, letting the magic pulse through me. It felt like an electric current. Brilliant light emanated from my hands and washed over the patch of land. I concentrated harder and increased the intensity until the vampires' skin crackled and burned. Finally, they crumbled to dust, and the pieces scattered across the bog.

Silence descended upon us. I closed my hands and lowered my arms to my sides.

My crew joined me at the bog's edge back in human form and fully clothed. They'd come prepared.

"Somehow, I don't think it was an accident that no one apprised me of this plan." Lord Doran would be furious when he discovered the rangers were missing and presumed dead. His retaliation would put us all at risk.

"I thought you knew," Bear said, throwing a dirty look at Hugo.

"And you thought I would approve of this? Do you even know me?" I snatched the arrows from Hugo's quiver and placed them in my own. "Don't even think about touching my weapons again, or you'll find yourself on the wrong end of one of them." I waved a hand at the dead horses. "You can clean up this mess. I'm going back to the hideout."

I walked toward the Beast, unwilling to give the carnage another look. I'd have nightmares about those poor horses.

Bonnie chased after me. "You're wrong about this, Aster. Hugo is willing to take a hard stance, and we should support that. We need to stop playing nice with vampires. They aren't our friends."

I whirled around to face her. "I'm well aware of our relationship to vampires, Bonnie."

She glared at me. "Exactly my point. Doran and his rangers killed half your coven and destroyed your home. Your family. Yet you continue to handle them with kid gloves."

"Because I like to think I'm better than they are, and that means not condoning massacres or senseless violence."

She gestured to the vampire's head in my quiver. "And that's supposed to be a symbol of your decency?"

"You know why I killed this one." It had been self-defense. Afterward, I decided to use his head as a symbol to others to show we were down but not out. It helped that the ghastly head intimidated any vampires I happened to encounter.

"We all have our reasons," Bonnie argued. "Just because they're yours doesn't make them better."

"Reasons matter, Bonnie. Reasons for killing. Reasons for stealing. Not all are created equal, and not all deserve to be given the same weight." That's why, once upon a time, there were laws that separated murder charges into degrees. Not all homicides deserved the same punishment. Granted that was a different world when humans were in charge, but they were rules I still tried to follow in my own way. I didn't need a law to tell me that what happened in the bog was flat-out wrong.

"We should be doing more than petty theft!" Bonnie yelled, but I'd already started toward the Beast. I was furious with the entire crew. Although they hadn't directly disobeyed, they knew how I'd react to their plan, which was why they'd kept it hidden from me. I was disappointed that Bear thought I would've approved. It was an insult to my character.

I was relieved Scarlet hadn't been involved. Hugo must've planned this insubordinate act carefully. He knew Scarlet wouldn't have kept a secret from me. She'd be livid when she found out.

That made two of us.

I increased pressure on the pedal, bouncing over roots as I zipped toward the hideout. There were too many external threats at the moment. I couldn't deal with internal threats as well. We were either a team or we weren't, and if we weren't—well, I couldn't bear the thought of it.

When I returned to the hideout, I found Scarlet talking to Hattie by the storage unit.

"Did I miss an adventure?" Scarlet asked.

"We need to talk."

My serious tone didn't escape her notice. Scarlet excused herself, and we climbed to her tree house at the edge of the hideout. Her home was cozier than mine, with knickknacks and personal mementos. A wooden owl that Tyson had carved for her took pride of place on the lid of a trunk. She loved owls. I didn't own anything that I'd be sad to leave behind. I learned that lesson during the purge.

"What happened?" she asked.

I told her about Remy's Bog. The lines across her forehead deepened with each revelation.

"Everybody knew except me, you, and Hattie. Bear claims he thought I knew."

"Do you believe him?"

I shrugged. "Doesn't matter. What matters is what they did."

Scarlet plucked the fabric of her woolen blanket. "What do we do about it? We can't function as a team if there are secrets."

"I know." I felt mildly uncomfortable with that exchange, knowing I kept a secret of my own, but it wasn't the same.

Before we could reach a conclusion, Hugo's voice reached us from the ground. "Aster, can I talk to you?"

I peered out the open doorway. "Whatever you have to say, you can say to both of us."

"Let's go down," Scarlet suggested. "I don't want him in my personal space."

I understood. Our tree houses were our sanctuaries. The only place we could shut out the rest of the world and be alone with our thoughts.

We climbed to the ground. Hugo was alone. He held up a bag of potatoes.

"Peace offering," he said.

I accepted the offering, but only because I liked potatoes. "We're only as strong as our weakest link. You weakened us today with that stunt."

He lowered his gaze to the dirt. "I know. I'm sorry. It won't happen again."

"What made you change your mind?" Scarlet asked.

"We discussed it on the walk back here," Hugo explained. "Bear argued your position, Aster. I know what it took for you to use your magic that way." He shook his head. "It can't have been easy."

"No, it wasn't, but the damage was done, so I didn't see a choice. We're already dealing with a mysterious sickness. We didn't need to throw a vampire massacre into the mix."

"The Green Death," Scarlet chimed in. "That's what people are calling it."

I frowned at her. "It has a name?"

She shrugged. "It does now." She pinned Hugo with a hard stare. "Why did you do it?"

"Why do we do any of the things we do?" His gaze slid to me. "You play with them like it's cheap entertainment. I don't care about being entertained. I care about freedom from vampire rule."

Guilt seeped into my pores. He wasn't wrong. My interactions with rangers were more about scoring points and getting under their skin. They weren't about advancing a particular cause. Still, senseless violence wasn't the answer.

"Aster is the Hooded One and that makes her *our* number one, and I'm her second-in-command," Scarlet said. "If you can't accept that, then I suggest you look for another group to join."

He dragged a hand through his thinning hair. "I said it won't happen again. You might want to give your speech to Bonnie, though. She doesn't seem as contrite."

No doubt.

"For someone desperate for a baby, Bonnie sure seems to have a death wish," Scarlet remarked.

"She's tired of living like this," Hugo explained. "She wants to raise children in a pack, as part of a community, but as long as vampires are in charge, that won't happen."

"We're all tired of living like this," Scarlet shot back. "We still can't put our own needs ahead of the group."

"What about the Ghost Pack?" Hattie interrupted.

I whipped around to see her standing behind me. "How long have you been listening?"

"Long enough."

Scarlet sighed. "There's no Ghost Pack, Hattie. It's a myth."

"There've been sightings of them in the Yukon," she argued. "They're hundreds strong."

"It's a nice fairytale, but I'll believe it when I see it," Scarlet said. "Besides, large pack. Small pack. Doesn't matter. As long as the world is trapped forever in midnight, vampires have the advantage."

"Your kind can see in the dark as well as they can," Hugo countered.

Scarlet brushed off his comment. "It isn't as simple as night vision."

I had no opinion about the Ghost Pack one way or the other. If they wanted to help build a better world, terrific. I'd welcome them with open arms. Like Scarlet, though, I was skeptical of their existence.

Hugo steepled his fingers, thinking. "How about this? I'll take both of your watch shifts this week as penance."

"Two weeks," Scarlet said.

"Done."

"Let's go to the campfire," I said. "I want to address everybody as a group." I couldn't let this issue fester.

Once the rest of the crew assembled by the campfire, I launched into my speech. "If we expect to survive in The Wild, we need to have each other's backs. Planning secret attacks won't be tolerated." Bear tried to speak, but I talked over him. "I don't care who was told what. If something doesn't square with how we typically do things, it's your job to question it. Anybody who can't follow orders should pack their things and go."

"And if you do go," Scarlet added, "we expect you to continue to keep Aster's identity secret for the sake of ... well, everyone."

Bonnie's mouth stretched into a thin line of displeasure. I'd made my point.

"We'd never divulge your secret," Bear said. "They wouldn't even be able to torture it out of me."

"They'd have to kill me first," Tyson chimed in.

Bonnie was noticeably silent. I couldn't let the moment pass unacknowledged. It was a threat to my leadership role.

I put her on the spot. "Bonnie, how about you?"

"Of course," she said. There was an edge to her tone I didn't like.

"I understand your position," I told her. "I know you think I don't, or that I'm too weak to take more serious action, but I promise you it isn't that simple."

Without warning, she turned away from me and wretched. I jumped back to avoid the fallout.

Bear slid closer to her. "Are you okay?"

My mind went straight to the Green Death, even though my rational brain knew vomiting wasn't a symptom.

The werewolf straightened and used a folded cloth from her pocket to wipe her chin. "I guess this is a good time to tell you all that I'm pregnant."

Bear whooped loudly and engulfed his partner in a tight hug.

"Congratulations." I felt mildly guilty for not saying it with more enthusiasm.

Hattie stared at the ground. Maybe this development would finally end her one-sided crush.

"Do we need to get anything for you?" Bear asked, his hand placed protectively over her stomach.

"Peppermint tea has helped."

"On it." He vaulted over the seat.

Scarlet raised a hand. "I'd like peppermint tea, too."

"Peppermint tea for everybody," Bear exclaimed. Joy radiated from his face.

I wasn't sure what a baby would mean for the crew. Whether they chose to stay or go didn't matter. Either way, things would have to change. My grandmother used to say babies were a blessing.

I wasn't so sure.

Chapter Six

The next day I returned to Berthold to confirm the rumor Scarlet had heard. I wasn't surprised by the outcome.

"My poor Xavier is dead." Lucinda Joyce sat at a wooden table with a cloth covering her nose and mouth.

"I'm so sorry." I reached across the table to give her hand a gentle squeeze.

"I had to watch two men in masks carry my husband's body out of the bedroom on a stretcher." She grimaced. "He had those green sores all over his skin. Even his hair was streaked with greenish slime." Lucinda stifled a sob as she relived the memory.

"That had to be difficult for you."

"I feel like I'd be better off burning down the house than trying to scrub it clean of whatever that was."

"What will they do with the body?"

She buried her face in her hands. "Torch it. Can't risk infecting anybody."

They'd have to choose somewhere far enough from civilization. They couldn't risk the stench spreading to other areas. Right now, it was unclear whether the disease was airborne or how Xavier became infected.

"Could it have been something he ate?"

"Doubtful. He ate the same as us. I packed his meal and sent it with him to work."

"You mentioned he was a cobbler."

The way she nodded made it seem like her head was heavier than a boulder. "Worked out of a stone barn on the outskirts of Whitehead. There's no road sign, but everybody knows it as Stonybrook Lane."

"Thanks. I'll take a look there, if you don't mind."

"His apprentice will be able to show you around. I guess Jackson will be the cobbler now." She wiped away a stray tear. "He's a clever boy. He'll learn fast."

It seemed he had no choice.

I dropped by the Dancing Dragon on my way to Whitehead. I felt in need of a friendly face or two. It was relatively empty at this hour. I hopped on a stool and waved at Glenn, who was busy serving two regulars at the end of the counter. He refilled their pint glasses and ambled over to me.

"Twice in one week? How'd I get so lucky?"

"Because Lucinda and Xavier were unlucky."

His face darkened. "Ivan and Smith were in here before they went to collect the body. They looked ridiculous in those masks."

"If you smelled what I did, you'd understand."

"No, I get it. My wife said it's smart to take precautions, so they don't breathe in the vapors."

"She thinks it's airborne?"

"Well, she isn't an expert in science or anything. What she does know is history, and she says this seems a lot like the Black Death. That's why people have started calling this the Green Death."

"How are they similar?"

"The plague killed its victims within two days. There was a high fever and terrible sickness. Did you know nearly half the population of England was cut off from the world in less than a year?"

"Half?" I wasn't sure of the population then compared with now. Either way, it was a lot of people.

He made a chopping motion with his hand. "Whole communities were wiped out. Didn't matter if you were rich or poor. The plague didn't recognize class or species." He picked up a cloth and dried a glass pitcher. "There was an upside, though. On account of so many dead, workers were in short supply. They started to demand a living wage, and they got it."

I considered his words. "You think the Green Death might spread to vampires?"

"According to Rita, it's only a matter of time, and we both know she's the smart one in the family."

"Does she have any advice on how to avoid catching it?"

He cast a furtive glance around the empty pub. "She's making the kids stay indoors for the foreseeable future. Windows closed. Company limited."

"But you're keeping the pub open?"

"Have to, or we'd die anyway."

"Anyone else sick that you've heard?"

He shook his head. "The twins asked if we should sage the place or hang hawthorn on the door. I don't have any experience with that sort of thing." He eyed me. "What do you think?"

"I wish I knew. Do whatever makes you feel more at ease, but don't expect it to be a miracle cure."

"Can I get you anything?"

"No, thanks. I'm heading over to Stonybrook Lane to see Xavier's apprentice."

"Jackson's a good boy. I don't envy him, though. This'll be a tough transition for him."

"Tough for Xavier's family, too."

"The village will help them out. We look after our own."

The coven used to say that. A fat lot of good that did us in the end.

Stonybrook Lane was on the outskirts of the village. The narrow road was indicated by a row of stones on either side and within range of a babbling brook.

"A little on the nose," I mumbled to myself as I approached the stone barn. A bicycle leaned against the exterior, and the double doors were wide open. Good. Jackson was here.

The stench hit me before I made it to the doorway. I covered my nose and mouth and forced myself to enter. The interior light was on, illuminating a young man slumped over a table. His eyes were closed, and his face was covered in lesions that oozed the same green liquid as Xavier's skin.

"Jackson?" I didn't expect an answer. Based on the number of flies, Jackson had died around the same time as Xavier, which suggested they were also infected at the same time.

I adjusted my cloak so that the hood covered my nose and mouth and tied the drawstring around the back of my neck. A pair of black boots rested on the table in front of him. The soles were worn and the toes scuffed. It appeared he'd been in the process of mending them.

Tears stung my eyes as I studied Jackson's lifeless body.

He must've been an orphan; otherwise, somebody would've noticed his absence.

I pulled on my gloves and lifted the half-eaten sandwich on the table. Flies buzzed around the remainder, and I swatted them away. A jug squatted on the corner of the table, along with an empty glass. I leaned over and lowered my hood to sniff the contents of the jug. Just water.

I returned the hood to its protective position and continued to investigate the interior of the stone barn. Big surprise, it mostly consisted of tools and shoes.

A silhouette appeared in the doorway. "Hello?"

"Don't come in," I yelled.

"What's going on?"

"Jackson's dead."

"Shit." There was a pause and then, "Did he manage to finish my boots first?"

I grabbed the pair of boots from the table and tossed them one by one at the doorway.

"That's too bad. With both of them gone, I'll have to head over to the cobbler in the other village," he said. He sounded more put out about the extra travel than the two dead men.

"Guess so." I walked closer to him for a better view. "What's your name?" Anybody with such a blatant disregard for human life was going on my mental list of people not to help. I could be petty when the situation warranted it.

"Ezra Hamish. Who are you?"

"Aster Goodfellow."

He didn't react to the name. Instead, he picked up his boots. "This smell is awful. You should tell someone to get rid of the body."

"Next on my to-do list."

Ezra left, and I did one more circuit of the barn before the overpowering odor won out. I didn't see anything out of the ordinary. It was likely that Jackson had been working despite feeling unwell, tried to force himself to eat lunch to keep up his strength, and succumbed to his illness. His youth was probably the reason he was able to function longer than Xavier, plus the fact that he had no one at home to insist he stay in bed.

I kept my hood across my face until I left the barn. Removing my gloves, I crossed the lane to the brook and splashed water on my face. The image of Jackson's youthful face would haunt my dreams. I'd witnessed my share of dead people, but there was something about a disfiguring disease that made death seem that much worse.

Three people. Same fast-moving illness. What we didn't want was an epidemic. A village of this size could be wiped out within a week.

I arrived in the heart of the village to alert the local healer to Jackson's condition. Mauve Kaminsky had the kind of cheeks that begged to be stuffed with acorns. She'd been a member of my coven before it was disbanded, and she'd known me since I was born. She also knew about my light magic, but like so many others, she was willing to take that secret to the grave, for which I was grateful.

"I'll have the body taken care of," Mauve said.

"People are calling it the Green Death."

"Yes, it's concerning," Mauve said. She tugged at a loose strand of gray hair as she absorbed the news. I still remembered when her hair was a deep chestnut and her face was unlined. To live long enough that she'd sprouted multiple gray hairs—Mauve was considered one of the lucky ones.

"Have you heard reports of similar deaths in other villages?"

She shook her head. "I'll send a few inquiries to be on the safe side."

"I think that would be wise." I dropped into a chair. "How do we defend against a disease we don't understand?"

She bustled to the kitchenette behind her and turned on a burner for the kettle. "It's a puzzle, sweetness." She turned to smile at me. "I remember when you and your grandmother would sit at her kitchen table with a giant puzzle."

I hadn't thought about that in years. Coven members knew we liked them, so whenever anyone discovered one, it would end up in the home of Maya Goodfellow.

"My favorites were the ones with cats."

Mauve chuckled. "Go figure. I swear you fed every cat in The Wild. You were like Snow White, skipping through the woods with a trail of felines behind you."

Stray cats were few and far between now. Their population started to dwindle during my youth and eventually reached the point where it was a rarity to see one outside of someone's home. People blamed vampires for their disappearance. There was a small community of ethical vampires in The Wild that avoided human blood but wouldn't be opposed to other warm-blooded hosts. I tried not to dwell on it.

Mauve poured hot water into two cups. "Ginger or lavender?"

"Ginger, please." My stomach was uneasy from the day's events.

She set a steaming cup in front of me and pulled out a chair to join me at the table. "Tell me everything you noticed. Maybe between us, we can figure this out."

A knock at the door interrupted us. Mauve swallowed the mouthful of tea that filled her cheeks and greeted the new arrival.

"Nathaniel, you and Caleb are needed again," she said.

Nathaniel grimaced. "Not another one like Wilton?"

"I'm afraid so. You'll need to take precautions until we know more."

I looked at Mauve. "You don't think you should examine the body this time?"

"Can't risk it, my darling. I'm the only healer this village has, and Frank isn't carrying his weight these days. As you well know, a healer can be the difference between life and death."

"What's the story with Frank? I thought he was reliable."

She blew out a breath. "Hell if I know. I think the work is getting to him."

I thought of Jackson's apprenticeship. "Are you training anyone to replace you ... when the time comes?"

She tugged that same strand of gray hair. "Are you calling me old?"

"I'm being practical."

"I know you are, Aster. It's one of your best qualities. It'll keep you alive longer, that's for sure."

Nathaniel approached us. "Got another mask? Last one's ruined."

"What happened to it?" Mauve asked.

"Threw up in it afterward."

"Can't say I blame you," Mauve said. "Try to avoid breathing in any noxious fumes. We still don't know what we're dealing with."

"We're doing our best. The fire makes it worse, though. The odor seems to carry for miles. I swear the smell followed Caleb and I halfway home."

Mauve drank her tea. "Then take this one farther away from the village. We don't want to spread it." She inclined her head toward a closet door. "I've got more masks and gloves in there."

"Any hazmat suits?" I asked. They were rare in The Wild, but they existed.

Mauve's eyes brightened. "As a matter of fact, yes. They've been in storage so long; I'd forgotten about them." She glanced at Nathaniel. "The coven kept a few on hand for magical experiments that could go awry. I managed to save a few after the purge."

While she directed him to the hazmat suits, I finished my cup of tea. By the time I slurped the last drop, my nausea had subsided.

"Do you have an extra suit for me?" I asked. If I intended to continue this investigation, it wouldn't hurt to add an extra layer of protection.

Nathaniel unfolded a yellow jumpsuit and held it against the length of his body. "This one's too big for you." He tossed the suit on the nearby sofa. "I've never seen anything like this sickness. Have you?"

Mauve and I shook our heads in unison.

"We've been fortunate to avoid deadly outbreaks until now," Mauve said. "We did have that flu epidemic when you were young, though. That was a scary time."

I stood and delivered my empty cup to the sink. "Rita and Glenn were comparing this to the plague."

Mauve sucked in air between her front teeth. "I wouldn't go throwing around words like 'plague.' It'll kick off mass hysteria."

"Can you think of any plants that might help with the symptoms?" Maybe if we slowed the symptoms of the next victim, it would give us more time to diagnose the disease.

"Green pus and sores?" Mauve shook her head. "I can

work on a tonic to be applied to the skin, but at the rate the illness progresses, it will take more time than we have."

Nathaniel returned to the table, now wearing the hazmat suit over his clothes. "Where's the body? I'll grab Caleb and head over." When I told him, he blanched. "The apprentice, too?"

"Afraid so."

"Did you check their supplies? Maybe it's some new polish they were using."

"And what? They decided to eat it?" Mauve asked in jest.

"No, but maybe it's potent enough that it seeped into their pores," Nathaniel suggested. "You've seen the lesions," he said to me. "You know how they look."

"It's not a bad theory, but I had a look around the barn, and I don't think it's the polish."

He tucked the face protector under his arm. "Then what?"

"I don't know yet, but I'm working on it."

"Glad somebody is," he replied. "We all know Lord Doran and the rest of the bloodsuckers won't do anything about it."

"You would think they would, considering you're their primary source of food," Mauve commented. "They're letting a fox in the henhouse when they rely on the eggs to live."

"Vampires don't always act in their own best interests," I told them.

Mauve wore the hint of a smile. "To be fair, I could say that about many of us."

Nathaniel picked up a second suit for Caleb. "I'll let you know when it's done." He left the office with a grim expression. I didn't blame him. What he was about to do was both unpleasant and dangerous.

"Is there any family to notify?" I asked.

Mauve's half smile evaporated. "No. Jackson lost his parents two years ago. No siblings or other relations."

"What happened?"

"Remember that monster attack outside Anchorage?"

"Unfortunately." The details had been gruesome. Twenty-two people died.

"Jackson survived. We thought it was a miracle."

It was moments like this that hope seemed illusory. Why let him survive a tragedy only to succumb to another one two years later? The universe had a lot to answer for.

"Send word to me if any unusual cases get reported to you. I'd like to see if I can identify any patterns."

"Yes, ma'am." Mauve sounded faintly amused by the request. To her, I'd always be the little witch that completed puzzles at my grandmother's table, albeit one with the rare ability to simulate sunlight.

"I wish I had more useful magic like yours," I blurted. I hadn't intended to say anything, but I felt so useless in a situation like this. What was the point of such limited magic? Yes, it was rare and powerful, but I would've been a much more productive member of society if I could make healing tonics like Mauve.

"Don't be silly, my darling. Your magic is special. It protects us from greater harm from vampires. Our situation could be much worse if Doran and his goons weren't wary of the Hooded One."

"Maybe so, but it can't protect us from the Green Death."

Mauve's solemn gaze mirrored my own. "Don't be too hard on yourself. I'm not sure that anything can."

The door swung open, and two rangers entered. These two weren't dressed in armor. Instead, they wore the standard black and red uniform.

"Which one of you is Aster Goodfellow?" the blond vampire asked.

My bones chilled. "I am," I said slowly.

"We'll need you to come with us. Lord Doran's orders."

"Why?" They weren't slapping inhibitor cuffs on me; that was a good sign.

"His lordship didn't say," the blond vampire replied. "We were instructed to escort you to his office."

His office. Not the dungeon.

"I'll go, too," Mauve offered.

"No. Just her," the vampire said.

I considered fighting, but I got the distinct impression I wasn't in immediate danger. The vampires were far too casual in their approach. They didn't even brandish any weapons.

I maintained a neutral expression. "Fine. Mauve, I'll catch up with you later. If you could let Scarlet know I'll be late for dinner, I'd appreciate it."

"Better late than never, though, right?" the second vampire said. They both laughed.

Although I tried to remain optimistic as they escorted me outside, I found it hard to look on the bright side in a world of perpetual darkness.

Chapter Seven

The rangers escorted me to a Beast and unfolded a back seat. "Ooh, the VIP treatment," I said.

The blond vampire spoke to me over his shoulder. "This isn't the newest model. You should see the tires on that one. I have size envy, and that's not something I usually suffer from."

The driver looked at his companion and laughed. "Are you flirting with her?"

"No harm in it," the blond said. He tossed me a cheerful grin. "Is there? Who doesn't like a bit of attention?"

"She's human. You don't want to bother with that."

I didn't bother to correct his assumption.

"Save it for Doreen. You remember her. Red hair. Fangs."

"This one's got red hair," he said. "Must be my type."

"My hair is auburn," I corrected him.

"What's the difference?" he asked me.

"It's more of a blend of brown and red."

Pulling a face, he shifted to face forward again.

Lord Doran was based in Klondike, a settlement established at the start of the Eternal Night. Much of this region had been destroyed during the Great Eruption and rebuilt in a new way. Most official buildings in The Wild could be found in Klondike, along with the donation center.

The rangers delivered me to an office building. Out front, a House Nilsson flag flew at half-mast.

"Why is the flag at half-mast?" I asked the rangers.

"Because we lost a couple of House Nilsson officials in New York recently. Don't you people know anything?"

I shot him a quizzical look. "Lost them?"

"They were killed during an attack. I heard it was a group of wizards and witches called Trinity Group."

Another magical revolution squashed.

They escorted me to a corner office. The door was open, revealing Lord Doran Pope inside. The vampire rose to his feet when he noticed us.

"This is the one you wanted, my lord," the second ranger said.

"Leave us," Lord Doran ordered. "Close the door on your way out."

The rangers did as instructed. If only my crew were this obedient.

Lord Doran scrutinized me. "You're Aster Goodfellow?"

"Yes. How can I help you?"

"My lord. How can I help you, *my lord*?"

I gritted my teeth. "How can I be of service, *my lord*?"

The vampire seemed amused by the display of resentment. "Any relation to Maya Goodfellow?"

"She was a cousin," I lied.

"She was a real piece of work." He turned to the decanter on the console table and poured himself a drink. "Can I interest you in a drink, Miss Goodfellow?"

An offer of hospitality from the Thegn of The Wild?

"I didn't realize this was a social call."

"It isn't, but I'm having one. I thought it would be rude not to offer." He tasted the amber liquid in his glass. "Have you ever tasted whiskey?"

"No, I haven't." Spirits like whiskey are hard to come by in The Wild. We once ambushed a supply run that yielded a case of wine, but that was the closest I'd ever been to alcohol aside from beer.

"Then you're in for a treat. This is the smoothest whiskey you'll ever taste." He poured another one and handed the short, squat glass to me. "Bottoms up."

I stared at the amber liquid. I'd watched him drink, so I knew it wasn't laced with any poison or sleeping potion. I brought the glass to my lips and inhaled the interesting aroma. The liquid passed my tongue and slid down my throat. I felt a faint burning sensation as it settled in my stomach.

"So, what do you think?"

"Nice." Very nice.

"Now that I've fulfilled my duty as host, I'd like to hear what you know about the Green Death."

His request startled me. "That's why you've summoned me?"

"Yes. I'm hoping we can work together."

"Since when are you interested in working with anyone?" I tried to bite my tongue, but the darn thing kept moving anyway. Lord Doran acted as his own secretary, treasurer, and administer of justice. It seemed suspicious that he'd enlist my aid.

"I've lost three vampires to the Green Death in as many days, and several rangers are missing and presumed dead. I have a vested interest in this matter."

Three vampires. No wonder he was concerned. "What makes you think I know anything?"

"Because my rangers came upon two gentlemen burning a body. Your name was mentioned."

A lump formed in my throat. "In what capacity?" I'd worried this day would come, that someone might betray me.

"They said you've been trying to get to the bottom of the sickness. That you took it upon yourself in an unofficial capacity. Very admirable. Selflessness is a rare quality these days."

I relaxed slightly. The vampire's interrogation still made me nervous, but at least we were talking about the Green Death and not the recent spate of robberies or my magic.

"The healers can't risk getting infected," I said by way of explanation.

His mouth tugged at the corners. "And what? You've decided you're expendable?" He regarded me. "Or perhaps you think you're invincible. You seem the right age for that kind of folly."

"I want to help. If you saw how those men looked when they died, you'd understand."

Doran's mouth pressed into a hard line. "I saw how my vampires looked when *they* died. Vampires are generally impervious to diseases. I want to know why this one is different."

"This sickness is especially potent. A great unifier like the plague. It has no regard for class or species."

"Like the Black Death," he said in a thoughtful tone. "Now I see where the name 'the Green Death' came from. I hadn't put it together before."

"But you care now that some of your precious vampires bit the dust. Never mind the people who died before them."

The muscle in his cheek pulsed. "You think I wouldn't have cared? I wasn't aware of the seriousness of the situation."

I scoffed. "And you would've done something about it if you had?"

He took a step closer, towering over me. His broad shoulders seemed to fill the room. "Of course I would have. The Wild is my responsibility."

Despite every fiber of my being telling me to step backward, I stayed put. I refused to let him intimidate me. This was the type of moment when Scarlet's rational influence was needed. My pride was overpowering my need to see reason.

"Tell me what you need from me," he said. "My resources are your resources."

"Anything to preserve your primary food source, right?" The words tumbled from my lips before I could stop them. For someone who needed to remain hidden, I was certainly making myself memorable. I blamed my grandmother's genes.

He stared at me, the gold flecks in his hazel eyes burning with intensity, and I realized I'd stopped breathing. "It seems to me our goals are aligned in this matter. Are they not?"

"They are," I said with as much confidence as I could muster. My heart pounded at his nearness.

"You don't need to be afraid," he said quietly. "I didn't summon you to hurt you."

Defiance raised my chin. "I'm not afraid."

We seemed locked in a staring contest. I wasn't sure what I was trying to prove.

"Excuse me, my lord?"

He looked away, and I released the breath I'd been holding. A young vampire appeared in the doorway, clutching a clipboard against her chest. She wore a white blouse, a black pencil skirt, and a pair of black pumps. It struck me as the most frivolous outfit I'd ever seen. Who dressed like that in The Wild?

"What is it, Audra?"

"I'm sorry to interrupt, but Lord Birney wants you to know that the special supplies you ordered are arriving in Fairbanks on Thursday around 16:00. Would you like me to arrange a retrieval team?"

"Yes, thank you, Audra."

Special supplies? I wondered what they were.

Another vampire pushed his way past Audra and stumbled across the threshold. He continued toward us with unsteady steps.

Doran looked at him with disapproval. "Lord Birney, I thought you merely sent a message. I didn't realize you were actually back."

The earl cracked a smile. "It seems I ran out of money and goodwill." He wagged a finger at Doran. "You really ought to rule with a firmer hand. How dare they toss the Earl of the Outer Territories out on his ear."

Doran ran a hand through his dark hair. "Your time and energy are best spent in other ways. The king would never approve of all this hunting, gambling, and drinking."

"You only say that because you've never spent time with him." The earl's mouth split in a lazy grin. "And don't forget the womanizing. I'd say that's higher on the list than hunting for both of us. Although I suppose you could say they are one and the same." He offered me a mock bow. "And who is this charming creature?"

"None of your concern," Doran snapped. The intensity

of his tone surprised me. "We have a situation. Are you aware of the sickness that's sweeping The Wild?"

"The Green Death, yes. There was talk of it at the party I attended. You really should've been there. Plenty of pretty faces to admire." He cast a glance in my direction. "But I can see perhaps you've been preoccupied with one of your own."

Lord Doran scowled. "Audra, why don't you and Marcy escort the earl to his office? I believe there's a comfortable chair in there where he can rest."

Audra bowed her head. "Yes, my lord."

Lord Birney spun toward her and nearly toppled over in the process. "Yes, you and Marcy. Never too early in the day for a threesome."

"On second thought, Audra, I think the earl can manage on his own."

Lord Birney waved a hand in the air and stumbled out of the room without a backward glance.

Lord Doran pivoted to face me. "Apologies, Miss Goodfellow. The earl has a fondness for excess. He thinks The Wild is a behavioral suggestion. If it were up to him, our entire budget would be spent on lavish parties."

"And what would you spend it on?"

He savored the whiskey. "Regional planning and design."

Not the answer I expected. "Really?"

"I consider architecture the artistic side of town planning. It's the perfect blend of form and function."

"I can think of plenty of villages that could stand a facelift." Not to mention infrastructure.

His expression turned sour. "And if I had the budget, I would revitalize each and every one. I need the support of the House for something as extravagant as that. You have no idea how difficult it is to persuade the king of such needs when you live in a place called the Forgotten Land. I ask him every six months to approve a restoration budget, and every six months he ignores me without fail." He polished off his glass and set it on the table. "If nothing else, I'm grateful I was able to renovate some of the historic buildings in Anchorage."

"I didn't realize you were responsible for that."

He looked at me curiously. "Who else? Lord Birney?" He scoffed. "It was not without sacrifice. I had to agree to give up certain financial support in return."

I took another sip of whiskey and felt the warm liquid pool in my stomach. "Has the king ever visited here?"

Doran shook his head. "Never once. There was talk of sending his oldest son to take over for me at some vague point in the future, but he has yet to send any of his children to visit. Not that I blame him. It's a treacherous journey from the mainland. He wouldn't risk their lives by sending them here." His eyes locked on mine. "You seem ... perplexed."

My poker face was usually quite effective. I blamed the alcohol. "I feel like an honored guest."

"Would you rather I shackle you and send you to the dungeon? If you'd be more comfortable there, I'd be happy to arrange it for you."

I swallowed another mouthful of whiskey. "No, I'm good." I raised the glass. "To the manor born." I tipped back the glass and finished what was left. My head filled with a pleasant buzz.

"I take it you don't drink very often."

"What makes you say that?"

"You look as though you're about to fall asleep. I hope it isn't the company."

"Not at all. Is our conversation finished, my lord?" I asked. "I really should get back to my investigation."

"Yes. I'd like a report in a few days, even if you've learned nothing new." He walked to the open doorway and peered into the corridor. "Audra, would you escort Miss Goodfellow to the exit?"

"Of course, my lord."

As I left his office, it occurred to me that the missing rangers he mentioned were likely the ones from Remy's Bog. Guilt pricked my skin.

"Have a great day, miss," Audra said with a cheery smile. Her fangs took on a yellow hue under the harsh glare of the artificial lights.

"You, too." I burst through the doors and spilled into the fresh air. I took a moment to breathe in and out and steady my heartbeat. My reaction was a response to the stress of the situation, but there was a part of me that knew it was more than that.

I was attracted to that pointy-toothed bastard.

What was wrong with me? Lord Doran should repulse me. I should prefer the Green Death to his company.

And yet.

Although I resisted the urge to look over my shoulder, I could feel someone watching me as I walked away. I'd have to take the long way home in case he tried to have me followed. This whole visit could be a trap to uncover our hideout. Maybe he knew my identity and was using the Green Death as an excuse.

I walked at a slow and steady pace, casually checking over my shoulder every so often, but there was no sign of stalkers. Maybe I was being paranoid, and Lord Doran really did want my help. Still, I couldn't trust him, not even a little bit. He was the vampire responsible for the destruction of my coven and the death of my grandmother. I couldn't forget that, and I certainly couldn't forgive it.

By the time I arrived back at the hideout, dinner was cooking, and everyone was gathered around the fire. I inhaled the aroma of roasted vegetables, and my stomach growled in response. I'd been too stressed to be hungry earlier. Now I was ready to eat an entire garden.

Hattie was the first to pounce. "What was he like?"

"Tall."

"Taller than me?" Tyson asked.

I assessed the werewolf's height. "About the same."

Tyson grunted. "Can't shift, though, can he?"

"No, but his fangs are pretty impressive up close."

Tyson's face split. "Oh, are they now?"

"Intimidating, I mean," I quickly corrected myself.

"What did he want?" Scarlet asked.

"He's lost three vampires to the Green Death. He heard I was researching the human cases and wants to share information."

"Are you going to work with him?" Hattie asked.

"You mean *for* him," Bear clarified. "Nobody works *with* his lordship."

Scarlet cast a speculative look in my direction. "Is it wise? Maybe we ought to assign someone else."

"That won't be suspicious at all," Bear said in a sarcastic tone.

Hattie giggled. "I think it's pretty amusing that he's asked his Public Enemy Number One to assist him with a public health crisis without realizing it."

"Shows how ignorant he is." Hugo tossed a handful of sticks onto the fire. "He needs more effective intelligence."

"We cover our tracks pretty well," Bear said, slightly defensive.

"You mean the villagers cover our tracks pretty well," I said.

I told them about Audra's message.

"A special delivery to Fairbanks sounds like something we might want," Tyson said.

"I don't like that the earl is in the mix," Hugo said. "He's far worse than Doran."

That was my impression as well.

"While you were busy getting cozy with our enemy, I was gathering intel," Tyson said.

"If it involves a heist in Anchorage, forget it," I told him.

"Nope, it's the transport of valuables right here in The Wild."

We all looked at him at once.

"Whose valuables?" I asked.

"Your boyfriend's," Tyson said.

I groaned. "Stop. He's not my boyfriend."

"I think somebody has a crush," Hattie teased.

"Imagine having a crush on a vampire," Bear snickered. "You'd have to be messed up in the head."

"I don't know," Scarlet interjected. "Is it any different than a human and a werewolf? Or a witch and a werewolf?"

"I don't know any of those combinations," Bonnie said. "Do you?"

Scarlet averted her gaze. "No, but it doesn't mean they don't exist. We live in an isolated part of the world. We have no idea what's typical in other territories."

Bear wrapped his arms around Bonnie's waist and nuzzled her neck. "I can't picture being with anyone who can't shift. It would be like missing a piece of their soul."

"Well, it doesn't matter to me," Scarlet replied. "Love is love."

Bear planted a sloppy kiss on Bonnie's cheek. "Can't argue with that."

Hattie rolled her eyes at the display of affection and busied herself with the spit.

Scarlet must've noticed, too, because she murmured, "Speaking of crushes," and inclined her head toward Hattie.

The younger werewolf needed to find another outlet for her hormones. Bear was clearly happy with Bonnie, and now they were having a baby.

Bonnie yawned and gently pushed Bear's face away. "I'm full and ready for bed."

"Same," Bear said, patting his stomach. "I feel like I ran a marathon today." He shook his muscular legs. "Sleep well, everybody."

I picked at the remnants of dinner on my kebab. I'd eaten enough, but I hated to waste any.

"What if I challenged her?" Hattie asked.

I laughed. "Challenged her to what? A duel? This isn't a pack, Hattie. There's no alpha. You can't 'win' Bear's affections by winning a fight."

"I could if we fight to the death."

I laughed. "Hattie, this is ridiculous. No one is fighting over a romantic interest. We have more important matters to devote our energy to. Besides, even a pregnant Bonnie would tear you to pieces."

"That's the truth," Tyson interjected. "She scares me, and she's half my size."

Pain simmered in her brown eyes. "You don't think love is important? What's the point of living? You might as well turn yourself in to Doran now and tell him who you really are."

"Shut up, Hattie," Scarlet said. Her face was contorted

in anger. "Don't even joke about such a thing. If we lose Aster, we lose the war."

"What war?" Hugo said, inching over to join our small circle. "Ambushes and robberies don't count as battles. They're not even skirmishes."

"We have to bide our time," Scarlet said. "You know that."

"Yes, let's wait until the sun returns." Hugo expelled a breath. "Then those vampires will see what we're really made of."

Hattie's gaze drifted to the tree house where Bear and Bonnie had retired. "If a war does break out, she could die."

"We could all die," Scarlet pointed out. "Stop wishing death upon your friends, and start directing that ill will at your enemies."

Hattie's lips formed a pout. "I'm going to bed. I've had enough wisdom from the elders for one night." She stomped past us and climbed the tree to her house.

Scarlet stretched her arms over her head. "I guess I'll turn in, too. It's been a long day."

"Sleep well," I told her.

Tyson moved to sit on the other side of me. "Can we talk more about this heist?"

"Yes, let's," Hugo agreed.

I listened as Tyson offered the details. "Why would they be headed north?" As far as I knew, there was nothing beyond this expanse of forest except wilderness and mountains.

"Sounds like there's been activity up there. Doran's been building a new stronghold."

"If the route you heard is correct, we can head them off at the river," Hugo said.

"There's no bridge there, which means they must be

traveling on horseback and not in Beasts." Tyson grinned. "Ask me how I know."

"Yes, we all remember how you destroyed the last Beast," Hugo said without amusement.

"I say we go for it," I announced. "We could use the money for more supplies." And I could distribute money to the families of the Green Death victims.

"Then I'd better get some shut-eye," Tyson said, vacating his spot.

"I'm on watch," Hugo said. "Forever, apparently."

The wizard and I remained in front of the fire in companionable silence. I listened to the sounds of the forest —the crackling flames, the faint songs of the insects, and the occasional hoot of an owl. They were soothing and familiar, holdovers from childhood when I still felt safe. That safety had been an illusion, of course, but I'd bought it hook, line, and sinker.

"Hattie's young," he finally said. "She'll mellow in time."

I wasn't sure I wanted her to mellow. There was something oddly comforting about a young woman more consumed by love than fear. Hattie wanted to find a partner in this world and live her life on her terms. It was a basic desire, really, and it saddened me that other needs had to take priority.

"I don't know. Maybe she has a point."

Hugo cracked a smile, a rare sight, indeed. "Is there a gauntlet you'd like to throw down? A King Arthur you'd like to challenge for the hand of Guinevere?"

"I have too much responsibility to worry about personal relationships. I'll leave that to the rest of you."

Hugo snorted. "I don't have the energy for a relationship. It takes everything I have to be a productive member of this crew."

I cut a sideways glance at him. "Good. Not good that you don't have the energy for a relationship, but good that you're committed to us. You're the only other magic user in the group." As much as he aggravated me, I needed Hugo. The only spells I could cast were ones that had already been performed by someone in my direct bloodline. I didn't have the ability to conjure new ones like Hugo.

"Of course I'm committed. Vampires destroyed my home. They've wrecked my life. There isn't a worthier cause to devote my life to."

I nodded in agreement.

"Still," he continued, "it would be nice to have nothing more to worry about than whom I wanted to marry."

We both laughed.

"Another time, another world," I said. A world where my family didn't die too soon. A world where I didn't have to hide my true self.

"I'll put out the fire if you want to get some sleep."

"Thanks. I appreciate that." I rose to my feet and realized how heavy my body felt. I needed sleep more than I'd been willing to admit. "Pleasant dreams, Hugo."

"Sleep soundly, bright flame."

Warmth spread through me. Nobody had called me that in a long time. My father had given me the nickname, once they'd learned what I could do. It wasn't safe to use the nickname anymore. It was too much of a giveaway.

I trudged toward my tree house and made the arduous climb to bed.

Chapter Eight

"Does anybody know anything about this secret stronghold?" Bear asked. "This is the first I'm hearing about it."

"It's probably in response to the Green Death," Scarlet said. "He's probably got supplies headed this way too. We should keep our ear to the ground for that transport."

"Maybe the special supplies coming into Fairbanks are for this outpost," Tyson suggested.

I frowned. "This place already has to be built. He isn't going to send valuables to a construction site."

Bear folded his arms and kept his focus on the riverbank. "I guess that explains this bridge that wasn't here before. Probably built it in order to transport materials to the site."

"When would he have built any of it?" Hattie asked. "We would've noticed materials being dragged halfway across The Wild. Knowing Doran, it isn't some small, rustic cabin."

"How could we have missed it?" Bonnie lamented. "We're wolves, for crying out loud."

"I suggest we worry about this later," Scarlet said. "Unless they're running behind schedule, they should be here any minute."

We remained crouched behind a hill. I started to think about how much the valuables might be worth and how we could sell it without attracting attention. That was one of the difficulties of living in The Wild. We didn't have many options when it came to selling off merchandise. Cash was better but not always feasible.

"My knee is bothering me again," Bear complained.

Scarlett grunted. "When did you turn eighty?"

"I'm a burly guy. My knees take a lot of flak."

The sound of an engine silenced us. I peered out from behind the hill to see a Beast coming to a halt at the river's edge.

"I guess this explains why there's a bridge here now," Bear murmured.

"Only one Beast?" Scarlett whispered. "Way to make it easy for us."

I observed the vehicle, still hovering at the entrance to the bridge. "Now that you say that, it does seem strange. If they're transporting valuables, why not give them more protection?"

"Probably because no one is supposed to know about it," Bear said. "We got lucky."

The vehicle finally started to cross. We waited until the Beast reached the middle of the bridge to mount our attack. Hugo passed a ball of twine to Tyson.

"Smart man," Tyson said, winding up his arm and throwing the ball to the middle of the bridge.

Orange smoke exploded from the device. The driver hit the brakes, causing the vehicle to fishtail before crashing into the side of the bridge.

We jumped into action while the vampires were still stunned. Two more vehicles approached the bridge behind, each one teaming with vampires.

"Shit," Bear said. "I guess that's why the first one was stalling. Waiting for the others to catch up."

"You wanted more protection," Hattie said. "Here it is."

Tyson growled. "Is this a setup?"

"If it is, you're the idiot who fell for it," Bonnie told him in her usual charming fashion.

"I don't think so," I said. "They seem surprised to see us." Regardless, I didn't want this ambush to be for nothing.

Tyson grabbed the driver by the collar and shook him. "Where are the valuables?"

Drawing my bow, I sprinted toward the other two Beasts to hold them off. The rangers weren't dressed in armor. They were lucky there was no poison on these arrows.

Hattie joined me with a crossbow.

I glanced at her. "Who gave you that?"

"Tyson."

I'd have words with him later. Hattie wasn't proficient enough to use a crossbow.

Arrows whizzed at my opponents in quick succession. They took refuge behind their vehicles. Some protection squad.

I heard a splash and turned to see that Bear had pushed a vampire off the bridge. Tyson held up a gold necklace with a blackish-purple pendant. The remaining vampire tried to swipe the necklace from him and a struggle ensued. They toppled over the side of the bridge and plunged into the water.

"Somebody help Tyson!" Scarlet yelled.

I understood the reason for her panic. The werewolves in our crew weren't known for their swimming skills.

I looked around and realized I was the only one capable of going in after him. I perched on the guardrail. Before I could dive, the bridge shook violently. I fell backward, hitting my shoulder on the nose of the Beast. That was going to bruise.

I scrambled to my feet and peered at the water. Tyson had managed to swim underwater to the opposite bank. I spotted the gold necklace glinting in his hand. Way to go, Tyson.

The bridge trembled again, which was good because the other vampires had decided to advance on us.

"We need to get off this bridge now," Scarlet said.

Bear and Bonnie were too busy charging the vampires to heed her warning. Scarlet grabbed Hattie by the hand and ran. I reached land as a giant geyser erupted from the river. Water splashed over the bridge and washed away those who remained on it.

"Bear!" Hattie screamed.

But all I could think about was Bonnie and her bean.

Water continued to spout from the middle of the river, and a bulky figure emerged from its depths.

Scarlet pushed Hattie behind her. "What in holy hell-fire is that?" she yelled.

The creature was like no water monster I'd ever seen. Despite a reptilian head and body, it stood upright. Its legs and arms looked as though they were designed to live on land. It pulled the water aside with giant clawed hands and waded to the middle of the bridge. With each step, water rippled, and the ground trembled. It closed its hand in a fist and punched straight through the bridge. Beams of wood flew in all directions. The Beast dropped into the river. I was sure Tyson would've laughed if the situation weren't so dire.

My gaze shifted to locate Tyson. The werewolf stood helplessly on the opposite riverbank, now wearing the necklace. Two vampires swam toward him. Apparently, they were more interested in reclaiming the necklace than fighting the monster. Then it struck me. The monster's hide was the same blackish-purple of the stone.

"It isn't a monster. It's a demon," I said.

"How can you be sure?"

"Because I think it was summoned."

"Who would summon that thing?" Hattie asked.

"It's the necklace Tyson has. It's an amulet." And I had a pretty good idea where the vampires got it.

"I need you to whistle," I told Scarlet. Her skills were far superior to mine.

She let loose a shrill whistle. When the demon pivoted to face us, I pushed out my hand to blind it. The demon jerked to the side, momentarily disturbed by the light.

Bear and Bonnie appeared behind us, soaking wet. I'd thank the gods later.

"What is that thing?" Bear asked.

"Calamity demon," I replied.

If I was right, this was the same calamity demon that had been captured by the coven fifty years ago. My grandmother had spoken of its arrival in the village. They'd managed to capture it, but they couldn't kill it. The solution had been to trap it in a stone, but a dip into the chilly river must have released it from its prison.

"How do we kill it?" Bonnie asked.

"We can't," I said.

Scarlet smirked. "Terrific. What do you suggest then? Invite it to tea?"

"Maybe a bouquet of flowers?" Bear added.

The vampires must've confiscated the necklace during their destruction of our village and never bothered to research its origin. Now it was being transported to some new stronghold in the wilderness, along with Lord Doran's other treasures.

"Where's Hugo?" I asked.

Bear pointed to the hill where Hugo was lobbing magic bombs at the vampires as they attempted to climb out of the river.

"We need Tyson," I said. "He's got the necklace."

Scarlet began waving Tyson over. The werewolf had managed to dispatch the vampires, but there was still no bridge. Not to mention the demon itself, currently making short work of the vehicle that had fallen in the river. The demon tossed the Beast against the side of the hill and broke it into pieces.

"What do we do?" Bear asked. "I don't want to be that 4x4."

"We need to trap the demon back in the stone," I told them.

Bonnie snorted. "And how do you expect us to do that? We're werewolves."

And my magic was limited. Fortunately, I had a genetic advantage. If my grandmother was the one who conjured the spell to banish the demon, then I should be able to access the spell. I couldn't produce one in its original form, but I should have enough Goodfellow magic in my blood to be able to piggyback off an existing one.

"I might be able to do it."

The ground shook again, and large rocks skidded down the mountainside and rolled straight into the surviving Beast. It rolled into the river and sank.

We urged Tyson to cross the river. He managed it once. He could do it again. Without that necklace, we were doomed.

Tyson seemed unwilling to enter the water.

"We can't let that demon leave this area," Scarlet said. "If it gets anywhere near a village, it'll be catastrophic."

"They don't call it a calamity demon for nothing," I said. If I couldn't get Tyson to come to me, then I would have to go to him. I turned to my companions. "Cover me."

I didn't wait for a response. I dove into the water and swam. After a few lengths, I twisted to see vampires trailing me. If they'd bothered to learn anything about the valuables they carried, they would have known the risks. Dangerous when wet, among them.

Vampires might be stronger and faster on land, but they weren't skilled swimmers. It's a myth that witches and water don't mix. My mother once survived a vampire attack by hiding underwater in a well until the threat passed. She told me that story countless times in my youth.

Waves crested over me as I reached Tyson at the water's edge. The demon was on the move.

"Give me the necklace and shift."

Tyson didn't question me. He thrust the necklace into my hand and changed. I jumped on his back and spurred him on toward the mountain. When I dared to turn back, I saw the water level rising as the vampires in pursuit frantically tried to reach land. The calamity demon was summoning high tide. There was no sign of our companions. Hopefully they'd fled.

Rocks slid toward us as Tyson continued uphill. I needed to get a safe distance away while still retaining a vantage point. I wasn't sure what the range was for the spell to work, whether I had to be within a certain distance. We would have to guess.

I tapped Tyson's back and the wolf slowed to a trot. I tapped again, my fingers digging through his thick fur, and he ground to a halt. My feet slid to the earth, and I turned to face the river. There was no sign of any vampires now. The calamity demon was busy dissecting one of the vehicles it must've plucked from the river. The demon seemed fascinated by the four-wheelers. Good. Its curiosity would be my gain.

I held the necklace in the palm of my hand and concentrated on the stone. I pictured the demon inside. I knew there was an incantation for the containment spell, and I desperately tried to remember the words in Latin. The language was the forbidden tongue, and the coven had used it sparingly unless it was on behalf of House Nilsson, which was rare. It was one thing to have magic like mine that could be concealed. It was quite another to utter Latin phrases aloud and risk being overheard.

Not that it mattered right now. We were in an isolated location without witnesses. I was also doing it for the greater good. Scarlet was right, if this demon managed to make its way to civilization, people would have more than the Green Death to worry about. It could be the collapse of civilization, however little of it there was in The Wild.

I pictured my grandmother's face and called upon her spirit for guidance. I wanted to believe my ancestors were watching over me, although I was the one who could take on a ghostly form. I sometimes got the impression that my mother had resented me for having powers stronger and rarer than her own. Despite those brief moments of jealousy, I knew she loved me. She disliked my grandmother's determination to rebel against vampires because she'd wanted to keep me safe, to keep all of us safe, but my grandmother insisted that the coven would never truly be safe while under vampire rule.

I wondered what my mother would think of me now, picking up my grandmother's torch and continuing the fight on my own terms. My goals weren't as lofty as my grandmother's—I wasn't seeking to overthrow Lord Doran and his ilk, but I certainly didn't want to make life easy for them. It amused me to antagonize them, and I imagined my grandmother felt the same. "There's so little to enjoy about the world we inhabit," she once said. "Let us take joy where we can find it."

All at once, the words filled my senses. I curled my fingers around the stone and said, "i dici te."

The demon seemed to understand what was happening because it started moving toward us at a rapid pace. I wasn't wrong about the creature being designed for land. It was much faster now that it was out of the water.

"Hurry up," Tyson hissed.

The earth shook.

I repeated the spell over and over.

"Are you sure about this?" Tyson asked in a low voice.

The answer was no, but I had to stay focused on the task at hand. The ground vibrated, and a rock dislodged from the mountainside above us. Tyson knocked me aside before it reached us.

The demon had reached the base of the mountain. It raised its fists in the air, clearly intending to bring down the mountain with a vicious blow. To keep from losing my grip on the necklace, I slipped it over my head and repeated the incantation. Apparently, that had been the missing piece of the spell because I felt a tingling sensation on my chest as the amulet reclaimed its prisoner. My body jolted as the demon's essence was sucked into the stone. I fell backward and collapsed on the ground. My legs were too wobbly to stand, and Tyson had to carry me to the river where we reconvened with the others.

"Not a vampire in sight," Tyson said. "Just the way I like it."

Hattie turned to look at me. "How did you do that? I thought you couldn't cast spells."

"It's an extremely limited ability," I said. "My grandmother explained it like this." I tried to recall her exact words. "Picture footprints of family members that came before you. You can fit your feet inside of theirs and follow their path, but you can't leave any footprints of your own."

Hattie wrinkled her nose. "Sounds kind of sad. You don't get to chart your own course."

Bear clapped me on the shoulder. "Aster manages that part fine. She just doesn't need to cast spells to do it."

My gaze swept the area. "I don't suppose we were able to collect any other valuables." I wouldn't be able to sell the amulet.

Bonnie produced a small box and held it up for inspection. "Loose gemstones."

I exhaled and said a silent thanks to the gods. Loose gemstones were almost as good as cash. We'd be able to help the victims' families after all.

"Creating order out of chaos," Hugo remarked with a slight smile.

Tyson frowned. "What does that mean?"

Hugo patted the werewolf's back. "It means we're in a constant struggle to find balance, my friend. Some days we lose, but other days..." He nodded at the box. "We win."

Chapter Nine

I reached the peak of the mountain and dropped to my knees. My legs and back ached from exertion. I turned to gaze at the route I'd traveled. Only a single set of footprints were visible behind me. Mine. It had been a long way, but here I was.

My body twitched. Something wasn't right.

Two figures cut through the darkness, trailing behind me. It was too dark to see their faces. My magic itched to be released. I opened my palms and noticed the lines that streaked my hands were glowing with a golden light. My skin began to crack and peel as more light forced its way out of me. Soon the intense glow illuminated the landscape. It was beautiful.

I looked for the two figures on the mountainside, but they were gone.

Pressure started to build inside me. I wondered whether this was how a caldera felt before it erupted.

My body contorted, the movements now out of my control. A scream gathered in the pit of my stomach, gaining strength, and traveled up my throat until it ripped out of me.

I exploded like a star in its final stage of existence. A supernova right here on earth. There was no pain, but there was fear.

No, not fear. Terror.

I awoke drenched in sweat. At some point I must've kicked off the blanket. As I felt around the floor, I came to the realization that I'd kicked it out of the tree house. I peered over the edge, but it was too dark to see where the blanket had landed. Great. It was bad enough to have to climb down on the rare occasion when I had to pee. To have to retrieve a blanket was next-level aggravation.

I hopped nimbly to the ground and turned to see a silhouette.

"Looking for this?" Bear held up my blanket.

"Thanks." I took the blanket from his outstretched hand and wrapped it around my shoulders. "Couldn't sleep?"

"I'm on watch duty. Bonnie felt sick and asked me to take over for her." He motioned to the blanket. "What did the blanket do to warrant getting evicted?"

"Bad dream."

He grunted. "We all have those."

"This one was different." I'd had plenty of nightmares about the attack on the coven. I'd relived each terrible moment in excruciating detail. I envied the witches and wizards who'd been too young to remember.

"Want to talk about it?"

"Not really."

"That means you probably should."

I smiled. "You're very wise for someone called Bear."

He gestured to the campfire. "I've got a few embers in the ashes if you'd like to enter my office. No charge."

"How can I resist such a generous offer?"

We sat together on a log in front of the dying fire, and I told him about my nightmare.

"That's some heavy shit."

I laughed. "You think?"

"What do you think it means?"

"It's only a dream. Why does it have to mean something?"

Bear looked at me sideways. "Are you sure you're a witch?"

I played with the frayed edges of my blanket. "I guess it's an anxiety dream. That I'm afraid of being discovered."

"Maybe." His tone suggested he disagreed.

"What else could it mean?"

"No idea, but I'm thinking it'd be worth talking to an expert."

I debated whether I cared enough to dig deeper. "Anybody you'd recommend?"

"Have you heard of Poco?"

I shook my head.

"She's near Aurora Hot Springs. It's a bit of a trek but worth it."

"Is she a seer?"

"Not quite. You'll see what I mean. I met her when I was on my own. She's the one who set me on the path to this group."

"Then I suppose I'll have to thank her when I see her."

He chuckled. "That's up for debate."

"Thanks for the tip. I'll consider a visit."

"She likes flowers. If you see any along the way, make sure you take them with you."

"Any particular kind?"

"I don't think she's fussy. Hell, I think she'd be happy with a dandelion if that's all you see."

"I'll aim to do better than a pretty weed."

We sat in mutual silence for a few minutes. The nightmare had unsettled me, but I felt better now. Bear was right; it was good to talk to someone about it. It made a difference when I gave voice to my thoughts instead of keeping them in my head.

"Thank you, Bear. This conversation was exactly what I needed."

He stared straight ahead into the abyss. "Eugene," he said. "That was my given name."

I looked at him in surprise. "How did I not know that?"

"Because I haven't told anyone."

I slid the blanket off my shoulders and tucked it under my arm. "Then why tell me?"

"Because you shared something personal with me, and I know that's not easy for you." He shrugged. "Seemed like the right thing to do."

"You're very sweet."

The sound of footsteps interrupted us. I twisted to see Bonnie looming over us.

"Hey, what are you doing up, peaches?" Bear asked.

"I heard voices. I was wondering who was out here with you."

Even in the pitch dark, I could see Bonnie's rigid stature.

"Aster and I were dissecting her nightmare," Bear explained.

"If Aster is up anyway, why doesn't she take over and let you come to bed?"

I didn't want to have an issue with Bonnie, so I acquiesced. "Go ahead. Like Bonnie said, I'm awake anyway."

Bear gave me an apologetic look before rising to his feet.

"Sleep well," I called over my shoulder. I could hear Bonnie's terse voice as they disappeared into the void. As usual, she was overreacting. I had no interest in Bear, and he was smitten with her anyway, though I couldn't imagine why. To each their own.

The next day I focused my general frustration on an obliging tree trunk that I liked to use for target practice. Scarlet joined me, although her contribution consisted of handing me more arrows to shoot.

"Hattie had a crossbow with her yesterday."

Scarlet gave me a sidelong glance. "Was she supposed to come empty-handed?"

"She hasn't practiced enough. She could've hurt someone."

Scarlet smiled. "That's kind of the point."

I let another arrow fly.

"Nice shot."

I craned my neck to look at Hugo. "Thanks."

"What are your thoughts on a trip to Fairbanks?" he asked. "That's the conversation happening at the campfire."

"To intercept the special supplies?" I asked.

He nodded.

I accepted another arrow from Scarlet. "We don't even know what they are."

Hugo shrugged. "Only way to find out is to show up."

"Don't you think we should stay put? Fairbanks means overnight travel, and the Green Death is still running rampant here."

"Maybe it's run its course," Scarlet said. "The cobblers

worked together, so it makes sense that one might've passed it to the other, but Xavier's family is still alive."

"What about Devon Wilton, or the three vampires?"

Hugo grunted. "Who cares about vampires?"

Scarlet blew out a breath. "No clue. That's why I'm the brawn and you're the brains. Do you think it could be connected to the demon?"

"The calamity demon? No, it would've been benign while it was trapped in the amulet."

"Not the calamity demon. The one that killed Victor. Corentine." She handed me another arrow.

"I don't think so. Victor disappeared. No sickness or green puss. I think her sudden appearance is an unfortunate coincidence."

"Talk me through what you've learned up until now," Scarlet urged.

I could always count on the werewolf for sound advice. Mauve thought I was the practical one, but I gave the gold star to Scarlet when it came to rational thought.

I retraced my steps, starting with the sick but alive Xavier Joyce and ending with the discovery of Jackson's body.

"What do the three men have in common?" She shot me an aggrieved look. "Don't say a penis."

"Would I make a joke like that?"

"After two beers you would."

Okay, so drinking unleashes my salty mouth. There were worse flaws to have. "It's been only water today."

"So far," Scarlet said. "Give it time."

Hugo knocked on a tree trunk to get our attention. "Fairbanks?"

I glanced at Scarlet. "Thoughts?"

"Maybe we split the difference. Take half the team. I'll stay here with the rest."

"I'll stay," Hugo offered. "We should have one magic user with each team."

I nodded in agreement. "I'll take Bear and Tyson. I'll need the muscle."

"Hattie or Bonnie?" Scarlet asked.

I cringed. "Tough one. Gods, I wish Victor was still alive."

"We all wish that," Scarlet said.

I tipped my head back and swore. "I'll take Bonnie." If I took an overnight trip with her beloved Bear, he and I would never hear the end of it.

"Good choice," Hugo said. "We'll hold down the fort."

"Listen for any updates on the Green Death," I said. "I don't want to miss the chance to gather evidence. My new boss, Lord Doran, expects a report."

Hugo saluted me. "I shall make it my mission to dust for prints or whatever forensics teams used to do."

I narrowed my eyes at him. "They're not crime scenes. You have to look for scientific evidence."

Scarlet gave me a gentle shove. "Gather your team, bright flame. We'll take care of things here."

Hattie was the only one upset by the announcement. "You're leaving me?"

"I'm not leaving you," I said. "You're holding down the fort with Scarlet and Hugo."

Hattie pressed her lips together, and I could tell she was deciding whether to argue. "You're taking more than half the team," she finally said.

"Only because Victor isn't here to make it even," I explained.

Everyone fell silent at the mention of Victor.

Tyson raised a hand. "I can stay behind."

"Absolutely not. We need you. I have no idea how many vampires we'll be up against."

He shot Hattie a look as if to say, *Hey, I tried.*

"We'll bring you back a souvenir," Bonnie said.

Hattie's face twisted in a jealous rage. "I don't want a toy. I'm not a child!" She turned and ran from the campfire.

Bonnie's eyebrows crept up. "Could've fooled me."

"Are you sure you'll be okay for the journey?" I asked her. "How's the nausea?"

"I have a supply of ginger candies to suck on."

"Her vomiting's been better," Bear interrupted. "Trust me, I'm acutely aware of these things."

Scarlet and Hugo wished us luck, and Scarlet went to check on Hattie. We loaded our weapons into the Beast, along with food and water. I grabbed my golden cloak and tossed it over my shoulder.

"You're not going to wear it?" Bonnie asked.

"Not until we get there. No point in making ourselves a target before then."

"That's why you're the boss," Bear said, tapping the side of my head. "Always thinking."

"I think you'll find it's more to do with her magic," Bonnie grumbled.

Bear patted her belly. "And you'll be grateful for that magic in the future."

"I'm grateful for it now." Bonnie jumped into the back seat with the elegance of a cat. "I just wish she'd use it more often."

"Let's not give Aster a hard time," Tyson said. "We know her position, and we need to respect it."

Bonnie blew a raspberry but said nothing.

"Who wants to drive the first shift?" Bear asked.

Tyson's hand shot in the air.

"I'll ride shotgun," I offered. It would give Bear and Bonnie time to snuggle, or whatever expecting werewolves did together in the back of a 4x4.

Bonnie patted the seat beside her. "Come on, Papa Bear. Keep me warm."

"No need to tell me twice." Bear joined her in the back.

Suppressing my gag reflex, I climbed into the front seat and stared at the darkness ahead. It was going to be a long ride.

Chapter Ten

Fairbanks was once the city known as Alaska's 'Golden Heart.' Visitors flocked there to take advantage of the twenty to twenty-two hours of daylight in summertime referred to as the Midnight Sun. In wintertime, they swapped those long, glorious hours of sunlight for the aurora borealis.

But no more.

When I was younger, I longed to have the kind of magic that others in the coven possessed. Magic that was easily understood. Conjure fire. Make the trees dance. Fly on a broomstick. One day my grandmother found me crying because one of the wizards said I was as useful as a light bulb.

"The world wears a dark blanket, little one," my grandmother had said. "Don't you think a light bulb is rather important?"

"I'm a human light switch," I'd complained. "Where does magic like that even come from?"

That was the day she told me that she believed my talent was a form of sky magic. She shared stories of The

Wild before the Great Eruption, of the aurora borealis and the prolonged hours of sunlight.

"I believe all that brilliant light is now concentrated in you." She'd poked my tummy, which prompted a giggle from me.

"If I can control rays of light," I'd said, "then shouldn't I be able to disintegrate vampires?"

She'd looked at me with those intense eyes, so dark the irises sometimes seemed to blend with the pupils. "What makes you think you can't?"

It was in that moment that I grasped the potency of my magic and the importance of learning to control it, as well as hide it. My grandmother called me her 'golden girl' and tried to pass on as many lessons as she could before her death. It wasn't easy given the rare nature of my talent, but she did whatever she could.

"Aster," Tyson's voice broke my reverie.

"Sorry, what?"

"We're here." He motioned ahead.

The city skyline came into view. Buildings of various heights and widths lined the horizon. There were no tall buildings north of Fairbanks, so it was always an adjustment to find myself surrounded by them.

"If they're on schedule, then we only have an hour to prep," Bonnie said, always in business mode. I couldn't imagine her with a child. I pictured every stage of development as a box she couldn't wait to tick purely to move on to the next one.

"Let's cover all the angles." Tyson parked the Beast on a side street with little traffic and unfolded the tarp we'd brought to cover it. It was unlikely anybody in Fairbanks would recognize the stolen vehicle, but the risk was greater than zero, which meant taking precautions.

She climbed out of the Beast. "We should start with the plaza. That's our best vantage point."

"I would think a rooftop would be better," I said.

Bonnie was unable to contain her contempt. "Yes, because lingering on a rooftop isn't at all suspicious. We're not invisible, you know. That's their talent."

"We are when there's no light up there." I pointed to the top of the nearest tall building. Sure enough, it was shrouded in darkness. So dark, in fact, that the rooftop blended with the sky. Security wasn't so tight in Fairbanks that we had to worry about butterfly patrols. In this region, there weren't enough vampires with shifting abilities to spare and those who could change weren't exactly clamoring to leave their cushier locations to come to The Wild. They'd dubbed our area the Forgotten Land for a reason.

Bear's throat clearing meant he was about to agree with me, and he knew it would cause a problem with Bonnie. "Aster's right."

Bingo.

True to form, Bonnie's eyes blazed with barely repressed hostility. "Isn't she always?"

"It's a good plan. We'll be able to see what's happening below, but they won't be able to see us."

Tyson finally weighed in. Hallelujah.

"But we'll be too far apart to communicate," Bonnie argued. "How will we coordinate our movements?"

She had a point. We didn't have phones, mainly because the hideout wasn't equipped with a place to charge them. Phones tended to be useless in The Wild anyway. Satellites might work with more regularity in other parts of the world, but not here. Apparently, even technology considered us the Forgotten Land.

"I think we should have three on the ground and one

high," Tyson said. "Let's scout the area for the best triangle formation."

"I hate to question your expertise on shapes, but isn't that a square?" Bear asked.

"The three on the ground form a triangle," Tyson clarified. "The one up high gets the bird's-eye view."

No one objected, and we started toward the Golden Heart Plaza, a popular riverfront gathering place in the city where residents still congregated to celebrate special events. They continued to host the annual Midnight Sun Festival, even though there was no longer a summer solstice to celebrate. Some people believed that if they continued to honor the solstice that the gods would relent and return our precious sun.

We walked through the plaza and past the fountain statue titled 'Unknown First Family,' which was dedicated to past, present, and future Alaskan families. The plaza's central feature stood eighteen feet high with water that cascaded into a pool. Next to that statue was an even larger one that commemorated the Great Eruption.

"I never liked this one," Bear commented.

"Why not?" I asked. "It's a few calderas."

He tapped the base with his boot where statistics were engraved in the stone. "It reminds us how many lives were lost. I don't like seeing the numbers."

"It's mind-blowing," Tyson agreed.

At the opposite end of the statue stood a man in a dark blue skull cap. He looked almost as tall as the statue. Beneath the bulk of his clothing, I could tell he was ripped. Our eyes met, and he winked. I hated that my heart raced in response. He was hot, sure, but he was also cocky—a combination that should have me sprinting in the opposite direction. But I wasn't here to flirt. I was here to do a job. On the other hand, maybe if I succumbed to my hormones on occasion, I'd stop seeing Lord Doran as eye candy.

I turned to see Bonnie walking away, disinterested in the statues. Tyson trailed behind her.

"What's going on with her?" I asked in a low voice.

"Hormones," Bear replied, so quickly that I assumed he'd rehearsed the answer.

On second thought, maybe succumbing to my hormones was a bad idea.

I pondered the statue. "It's strange that they didn't include all the calderas. Think they ran out of materials?"

The werewolf chuckled. "I think they only included the ones that impacted this region."

Bonnie cast an annoyed glance over her shoulder. "Secrets again, you two? Maybe she's the one you should have a baby with."

Bear winced. "I really hope it's hormones," he whispered, "because if this is a permanent attitude adjustment..." He shook his head, leaving the statement unfinished.

I had no direct experience with pregnancy, and the only pregnant witches I remembered from the coven departed after Hecate's Revolt. I couldn't recall any details of their experience.

"I call dibs on that rooftop," Tyson said.

I followed his gaze to a five-story building across an empty parking lot.

"Any chance they'd travel by river?" Bear asked.

"That would be a pretty high risk," Bonnie said.

"Which might be exactly the reason to do it," Tyson interjected. "No interference."

"From people, maybe. Plenty of interference from sea monsters, though," Bonnie pointed out.

We wandered closer to the river to assess the options. Signs marked the entrance to pedestrian paths along the river and warned visitors to 'enter at their own risk.' The government claimed no responsibility if you were carried off by a kelpie or attacked by a giant squid that managed to make its way inland.

Tyson glanced uneasily at the river. "Anybody else feel like they want to run far in the opposite direction?"

I knew what he meant. Even in relative darkness, the ruddy color of the water made it seem as though the Chena River was flowing with blood.

"Somebody help!" a voice rang out.

All four of us turned at the same time to see a woman on the pedestrian bridge that spanned the river. She pointed at the water, her arm shaking.

"That thing's got Billy!"

What thing? I surveyed the surface of the water but saw nothing, not even ripples to indicate recent movement.

"Please help! He's all I have." The terror in her voice was unmistakable.

I sprinted to the bridge. "Where's your son?"

The woman frowned. "Billy isn't my son. He's my dog."

I glanced at the river. I was about to risk my life for a dog.

"What kind of dog?" Bonnie asked, appearing behind me.

"Does it matter?" the woman shrieked. "Hurry!"

I slipped off my cloak and dove headfirst into the water. I forced open my eyes to search for the dog and whatever monster had absconded with the canine. The water was murky, and I couldn't get a visual. I stopped swimming to tread water and maneuvered my hand back and forth in front of me, allowing light to splinter from my skin.

Gotcha.

The little white dog was in the jaws of an enormous horned serpent. Or maybe a water-based dragon. It was hard to tell. A round object glinted on its forehead. Weird.

The light reached its eyes, and the creature jerked away. Colorful circles lined its torso. I couldn't think of any monster that matched the description, which meant I couldn't identify its strengths and weaknesses. I'd have to wing it.

I swam toward the serpent, and its body undulated as it attempted to flee with the dog. The resulting current knocked me backward and I surfaced momentarily to draw breath before diving straight back down.

The monster surfaced briefly before diving back down. Maybe that would give the dog another chance to draw breath.

If I couldn't get in front of the monster again, I wouldn't be able to use my light to momentarily blind it. I'd have to use good, old-fashioned underwater fighting skills.

Terrific.

I grabbed the tail and hung on, allowing the monster to pull me through the water at a rapid pace. Once I had a firm grip, I slowly shimmied up the serpentine body. At close range, I could see how pretty the markings were. Pastel shades of blue, pink, purple, and green circled the monster's body. Every few feet, the serpent surfaced and attempted to jettison me. I held on for dear life until I finally reached the neck. I let go and propelled myself upward, grabbing the horns. I pulled myself forward and swung my body around until I was in front of the creature's face. Then I released a brilliant flash of light.

The monster's eyes shut, and its jaws opened, releasing the dog. I seized Billy and used the monster's head as a springboard to shoot to the surface. I didn't have much time to escape. Thankfully, the monster's aquatic acrobatics had landed us close to shore. Careful to keep the dog's head above water, I swam awkwardly toward land. Bear spotted me and waded into the water to carry the dog to safety, holding Billy upside down by the hocks and shaking him.

I crawled onto land and coughed up what seemed like a lungful of water. Bear had placed the dog on his side and was alternating between mouth-to-mouth and heart massage.

"He's alive," Bear announced.

The woman rushed forward, now in a long-sleeved shirt, and wrapped the dog in the sweater she'd been wearing.

"Oh, Billy. I don't know what I would've done if I'd lost you." She started to cry as the dog licked every inch of her face.

"Maybe next time don't walk Billy so close to the river," Bonnie advised.

The woman's hold on Billy tightened as the dog squirmed with excitement. "Normally I wouldn't, but today's the anniversary of my husband's passing, and every year I come and sprinkle a bit more of his ashes in the river." She stroked the dog's head. "It's one of our rituals, isn't it, Billy?"

The West Highland terrier responded by licking her lips.

The knot in my stomach loosened as I realized how much this dog meant to the woman. Billy was likely what kept her going day after day, and this ritual was an event she looked forward to, a moment each year that kept her connected to her deceased husband.

"I don't know how to thank you," the woman continued. "You're a lifesaver."

"Don't mention it."

The woman was still smiling when she turned to cross the plaza.

I squeezed the water from my hair. "My good deed for the day."

Bonnie handed me my cloak. "Why would you risk drawing attention to yourself like that? I get the desire to help, but you know better than that."

"The dog would've died."

Bonnie folded her arms. "When did you become such a bleeding heart?"

"What's that supposed to mean?" I snapped. I was quickly losing patience with Bonnie's negative attitude.

She gestured to my hood. "Your Robin Hood routine is to antagonize vampires, not because you actually give a shit about the common folk."

Bear replied first. "That's not fair, Bonnie. Aster goes above and beyond the call of duty all the time."

"That's my point. It isn't a call of duty for her. It's only a game. If it were a call of duty, we'd be plotting the next revolution instead of stealing their valuables for fun."

I balled my hands into fists to keep from slugging her. "Do you think I'm playing a game when I investigate the Green Death so that no one else dies from it? Or is that also merely to antagonize vampires? Did I trap the calamity demon because I don't give a shit about the common folk, as you so eloquently referred to them?"

She fell silent.

"I don't see you out there checking on villagers and gathering evidence," Bear told her.

A low growl emanated from Bonnie. "You're taking her side again?"

"Last time I checked, we're all on the same side," he said evenly.

Tyson tried to keep the peace. "Let's remember why we're here."

"Good idea." I didn't want to fight with Bonnie. We had plenty of enemies to contend with. No reason to add each other to the list.

We finally agreed on a plan and went our separate ways. As I crossed the plaza on my way to the building, I spotted the man in the blue cap watching me. If he were a vampire, I'd be more suspicious.

I found my way to the top of the five-story building that Tyson had originally claimed. Tyson stayed in the plaza. Bonnie walked farther along the pedestrian path and Bear watched the road that ran parallel to the river. No matter which direction the supplies came from, we'd have it covered.

No one seemed to notice me as I entered the building and walked straight to the staircase. The building wasn't crammed with people, but it was busy enough that I was able to blend easily.

I took the steps two at a time and continued until I reached the emergency exit at the rooftop. I held my breath and hoped I didn't set off an alarm.

I turned the handle, grateful when silence followed. I eased my way outside and left the door propped open behind me in case it locked automatically. That had happened to me on another job, and I did not want to repeat the experience of climbing down the side of a building. I was a witch, not a spider.

I crouched at the edge of the roof and surveyed the area.

Every few minutes I migrated to another part of the roof and scanned the horizon. Despite the city environment, it was peaceful up here. Not quite the crow's nest at home but pleasant enough. There was no sign of the mysterious man in the blue cap.

In the distance, a pair of headlights appeared. As the road curved, I spotted the body of the truck, as well as two more trucks close behind it. The convoy was coming from Anchorage.

I whistled once to let the crew know the delivery was imminent.

Fairbanks wasn't a particularly well-lit city, but there was enough illumination from the streetlights, head-lights, and flashlights to show me what I needed to see. I noticed a dozen or so city dwellers wearing old miner hats with the light affixed to the middle, sort of like the round object I noticed on the water serpent's head. They probably liked to keep their hands free in case they needed to fight off a monster or a robber. Come to think of it, miner hats might not be a bad investment. I looked at the row of shops below to see whether any might sell the hats, and that's when I noticed the rangers.

A gasp escaped me as I observed them spilling out of an unmarked pickup truck. They weren't part of the incoming convoy, nor were they meeting the delivery. They'd squeezed the pickup into a narrow alley between two small buildings and were currently lining up against the walls. These rangers were trying to stay hidden.

I craned my neck to check the proximity of the convoy. At their current rate of speed, I estimated they'd reach our location in five minutes. There was no way this was a coincidence.

Maintaining my crouched position, I turned back to the rangers. A few were loading rifles. My heartbeat jammed.

The realization hit me like a brick house. Lord Doran didn't haul me into his office to talk about the Green Death; that was only a diversion. His real purpose was to have Audra plant the seed of the supply delivery so he could find out whether I was connected to the Hooded One.

And, like an idiot, I fell for it.

It took me two attempts to whistle our emergency sound because I sucked at whistling. I ducked inside, tearing down the steps like my clothes were on fire.

I nearly collided with Tyson in the plaza.

"What's wrong?" he asked.

"It's a trap."

"There's no delivery?"

"Oh, there's a delivery, but Doran made sure to let me know about it. He's got rangers swarming the city."

Tyson whistled again to let Bonnie and Bear know to meet us at the Beast. We couldn't risk hanging around and being spotted. There was a chance that more rangers were on their way.

Tyson and I were the first to reach the vehicle. Bear was next, followed by Bonnie.

"Why are we meeting here?" Bonnie demanded.

"Because we have to call it off," I told her.

"Why? How big is the convoy?"

"Three trucks," I said.

She glanced in the direction of the road, as though she was still considering an ambush. "How many rangers?"

I climbed into the back seat of the Beast. "We need to go. Now. I'll explain on the way."

"I can't believe we traveled all this way for nothing," Bonnie grumbled as she dropped into the passenger seat.

"Because you had big plans otherwise?" Tyson shot back.

My shoulders slumped. "Bonnie's right. I wasted our time and nearly got us caught. I'm sorry." I told them about my theory.

Tyson banged his fist on his forehead. "I can't believe we let ourselves take the bait."

"It's my fault. I didn't give you all the information, only the tip about the supply delivery." I knew the reason, too. I'd been embarrassed by my response to Lord Doran and had omitted the bigger picture to avoid talking about him. And we nearly paid dearly for it.

"Hey, look on the bright side," Tyson said, settling beside me. "You saved a Westie."

"I don't know if that's a bright side," Bear chimed in from the driver's seat. "Bonnie seems to think you should only save a dog if it's over fifty pounds."

Bonnie glared at him. "I didn't say that."

"You implied it." He rubbed her shoulder. "Boy, I hope that bean of ours weighs more than fifty pounds when they're born."

Bonnie planted a sharp elbow in his side.

I rode in miserable silence. I was smarter than that. I'd endangered myself and my crew, and all because I was too distracted by Doran's display of interest and his gold-flecked eyes. I'd told myself not to trust what he told me, which should have included Audra's message. I'd never been more ashamed of myself.

Tyson leaned over and whispered, "Everything okay?"

"It will be." At least I'd figured out his plan in time and dodged a bullet. As far as Doran knew, I didn't bite, which meant he could rule me out as the Hooded One, and as part of the gang of outlaws. I hoped he viewed it that way anyway.

As the darkened landscape zipped past us, I spotted a sign affixed to a post. It took me a minute to realize what I'd read.

I poked my head between Bonnie and Bear. "Would you mind if we made a stop?"

Bonnie kept her eyes on the path ahead. "Where on earth would you want to stop between here and home?"

Bear seemed to realize our location. "Aurora Hot Springs."

"I wouldn't object to soaking in hot springs." Tyson stretched his bulging biceps above his head. "These muscles have been working overtime lately."

"What's the real reason?" Bonnie asked. Despite the suspicion in her voice, she turned the Beast around and made a right to follow the signs for Aurora Hot Springs.

"There's someone here I think she should meet," Bear said.

Bonnie's jaw tensed. "But not me?"

"Do you need any dreams interpreted?" Bear asked.

"No, but I wouldn't mind having my fortune told." She covered his hand with hers. "Would be nice to know if we're going to have a healthy baby."

Tyson nudged me and rolled his eyes. It seemed Bonnie's baby fever was annoying more than one of us.

"Pull over," Bear said suddenly.

Bonnie maneuvered to the side of the dusty road and rolled to a stop. "Did I miss a turn?"

"No, I saw wildflowers."

She smiled. "Oh, that's so sweet."

"Not for you. Aster needs them for Poco." He hesitated. "But we can pick a few for you, too, peaches."

Bonnie scowled and turned away from him. "Never mind. They'd die before we got home anyway."

I vacated the 4x4 and hurried to the burst of color. A mixture of purple and pink flowers grew in this one spot and nowhere else.

"Nature finds a way," I said, and plucked a handful from the ground.

The area grew more desolate as we continued to follow the signs. Skinny trees gave way to rocks until there was nothing except gently sloping hills. Finally, we reached an enclave of log cabins and a larger sign for Aurora Hot Springs.

Bear vaulted out of the Beast and breathed in the air. "Just the way I remember it."

Tyson patted his stomach. "I hope they have food. I'm hungry after all that unnecessary reconnaissance." He ruffled my hair. "I'm only teasing, Aster. Well, not about the hungry part." •

"I'll go talk to the front desk," Bear offered.

"I'll come with you." Bonnie was beside him before he could object.

"That woman's got issues," Tyson remarked, as soon as the couple had disappeared into the cabin marked 'office.'

"As long as they don't become our issues," I replied.

Tyson snorted. "Too late for that."

Chapter Eleven

The first thing I noticed about Poco was the deep purple color of her hair. Her skin was relatively smooth with little signs of aging, although she had the poise and general air of a wise woman.

"Poco, I'd like you to meet my friend, Aster," Bear said.

Poco seemed more interested in my offering than me. "I see you brought flowers. How kind."

I handed her the bouquet of wildflowers. She buried her face in the petals, sniffing each one. It went on so long I started to feel like I was intruding on a private moment.

Finally, she raised her head from the bouquet. "Thank you for the introduction, Bear. You may leave us now. Solange will have a meal ready for you and your friends."

Bear folded his hands in a prayer position and bowed slightly. "We're very grateful for your hospitality."

She waited until he left to continue talking to me. "Come and make yourself at home."

The cabin was cheerful and compact. There was a kitchenette in one corner and a small table with two chairs.

"Can I offer you a drink?" she asked.

"Water would be great." I felt like half the dirt between here and Fairbanks had ended up in my mouth.

She pulled a pitcher from the refrigerator and poured a glass of water. "Do you know what I miss the most about the world before the Eternal Night?" she asked, carrying the glass over to me.

"You were alive then?"

"Oh, yes. I'm older than I look."

"How? You're not a vampire."

"Fae blood."

I started to laugh, but the expression on her face gave me pause. "You're serious."

She nodded. "Everyone thinks the fae were a mythological species, but it isn't true."

I definitely fell into the category of 'everyone.' "Shouldn't you have wings or pointy ears?"

"I'm not full-blooded fae. The effects get watered down over generations." Poco turned to fill a vase with water and then removed a knife from the drawer. Slowly and methodically, she chopped off the ends of the stems.

"That's too bad."

She dropped the flowers into the vase and began to separate them from each other.

I guzzled my water in an effort to quench my thirst. "What was your life like before the Great Eruption?"

She looked at me with a puzzled expression.

"What?" I asked.

"You'd be surprised how few visitors ask me about it. They only want to talk about themselves, what I see for their futures."

"To be fair, that's the reason they come to see you."

"That's why you've come, isn't it? Yet you still want to know."

"I find the past interesting."

"As you should. It informs the present." She inclined her head. "More water?"

"If you wouldn't mind."

She retrieved the pitcher and refilled my glass. "I was a florist then. I had a beautiful shop in San Francisco, California. We created arrangements for weddings. Handmade bouquets for brides and bridesmaids." Her exhale was filled with longing. "Flowers made everything better. They elevated otherwise mundane moments to something special."

"What were weddings like then?"

"It depended on the couple. Some were extravagant affairs with ice sculptures and a live band. Others were simple. A barbecue in a family member's backyard." She shrugged. "Either way, they wanted flowers. Can you imagine a world where flowers grew freely and were so easily spared? Gods, I miss it."

"How did you end up here?"

"My husband and I were on vacation in Alaska when the supervolcanoes decided to blow their stacks." A faint smile touched her lips as she reminisced. "Carlos had always wanted to see the Northern Lights."

"Did he have fae blood, too?"

"No, he was human, and I never told him about me. He wouldn't have believed it anyway."

"What was your plan? Eventually he'd notice that he was aging more rapidly than you."

"We never got to that point." Her mouth turned down at the corners. "He died in the aftermath of the Great Eruption. Alaska wasn't a good place to be during that time. There weren't many places to seek shelter from the massive changes."

"I'm sorry."

She was quiet a moment and then said, "It was a long time ago."

"Did you ever find love again?"

"Not like Carlos." She tilted her head. "But I've had other companions who helped me pass the time." Her gaze raked over me. "You're a perky young thing. I'm sure you've experienced your share of suitors."

"I've had other priorities." I was more interested in talking about the fae. It seemed incredible to discover the existence of an entire race. This must've been how humans felt when vampires and other species started to emerge from the shadows.

Poco threw her head back and laughed. "Oh, darling. Trust me, you need to make time for amore. Love is what sustains you in times of great difficulty. Fae blood or not, I wouldn't have made it through the Great Eruption without Carlos. And I wouldn't have made it this long without the memory of him." She closed her eyes for a brief moment, as though conjuring his image.

"You were lucky to have met him."

"Sit down." She pulled out a chair and sat at the small table. "Tell me why you're here."

"I had a nightmare recently. Bear thought it might be useful to talk to you about it."

"Well, I must admit, I'm disappointed you aren't here to ask about your love life. Those are my favorite readings."

"Sorry to disappoint you."

She waved me off. "This is about you, Aster. Do you often have prophetic dreams?"

I blinked. "What makes you think it was prophetic?"

"Why else would you come here to tell me about it?"

"I ... I don't know."

She looked at me intently. "Describe the dream."

"Nightmare," I corrected her, and proceeded to share the details with her. "And then I exploded like a supernova."

Poco stared at me with a blank expression. Finally, she shrugged and said, "I've heard worse."

"I didn't realize we were playing the comparison game. I thought you'd help me understand it."

"I can give it a shot. Not all dreams are meant to be interpreted, though."

"What about mine?"

She pursed her lips, contemplating me. "Yours has potential." She cocked her head. "I can tell you're a witch. What I can't figure out is what you can do."

"Is that unusual?"

"For me it is. If you're an earth witch, I can usually smell the fresh soil. If you're a water witch, I smell the salty sea. You get the idea."

I couldn't tell her the truth. Too risky. "I have weak magic. Sort of like your fae blood. It's been diluted over time."

Poco arched an eyebrow. "So weak I can't even sense it? Interesting. Maybe that's tied to your dream. You're afraid that your magic will eventually kill you."

"An anxiety dream? Bear thought it might be more than that."

She broke into a smile. "One reading and he thinks he's an expert now, does he? Typical man." She snapped her fingers and motioned for me to hold out my right hand. "Let's see what more we can learn about this nightmare of yours."

"Do you only read palms?"

She kept her gaze fixed on my hand. "No. I have many

talents. Hmm." She tapped my other hand. "Let me see this palm."

I opened my left hand for her to examine.

"Fascinating. I've never seen so many lines on one pair of hands, especially one so young."

"What does it mean?"

She continued to gaze at my palms in wonder. "I think it means there are many roads to choose from, and you haven't committed to one yet."

"Any suggestion as to which roads to avoid?"

She peered at the left hand. "Are you sure you haven't met someone?"

"Like who?"

"A romantic interest." She tapped one of the lines on my hand. "I see one here, but it's complicated."

"Isn't it always?" I wondered whether she meant the awkward moment with Bear and Bonnie. That hadn't been romantic, though. Only misinterpreted.

"I see important women in your life."

"Scarlet and Hattie?"

She traced a line on my hand with her index finger. "These aren't women you've met yet."

"Why are they important?"

She scrunched her nose. "I can't tell. I see a triangle, but not a love triangle."

"What other kind of triangle is there?"

"Hell if I know." She closed my hands. "Your magic is stronger than you believe. It's possible that you're blocked because of trauma you've endured."

I jerked my hands to my side of the table. "You saw trauma?"

"I saw violence and loneliness. That suggests trauma." She studied my face the way she'd been studying my hands.

"What about your parents and grandparents? What kind of magic did they possess?"

"Why does that matter?"

"Like I said, the past helps inform the present."

"I didn't know my mother's parents. They died before I was born."

"What happened?"

"Sea monster. They'd gone with a party to gather supplies and were attacked." The irony of what happened earlier dawned on me. "Oddly enough, I had an encounter with a sea monster today."

Poco's eyebrows lifted with interest. "Just you?"

I nodded. "I've never seen anything like it. It was a huge sea serpent. It had these giant horns and a weird object lodged in its forehead. It looked like it was wearing a ceremonial headdress. Oh, and these pretty markings all over its body. It was like someone trying to put lipstick on a frog."

Poco's eyes widened. "You saw an uktena. How remarkable."

"I've never heard of it."

"I'm not surprised. They're uncommon creatures. They come and go from the underworld and rarely break the surface."

"This one must've been hankering for a dog kebab because it grabbed the little guy right off a bridge."

She looked at me in disbelief. "And you managed to extract the dog from it?"

"Not right away. I had to fight the monster underwater. No easy feat, let me tell you. My muscles will be aching tomorrow."

Poco gaped at me. "You fought the uktena and lived to tell the tale?"

I spread my arms wide. "Apparently. I guess it decided the dog wasn't worth the trouble."

Poco continued to gaze at me in silence to the point where I felt compelled to fill the empty air.

"The dog is okay, in case you were wondering."

Poco seemed to collect herself. "I'm glad to hear it."

"What's the shiny object on its forehead?"

"A crystal. It's said to yield its owner great power, although I'm not sure whether that's only a myth."

I laughed. "Either way, good luck taking it from him."

"You should use the hot springs before you go to ease your aches and pains."

"I would love to." I had no doubt the rest of my party were already there, enjoying the warmth of the water.

Poco scraped back her chair. "Let's try something else."

"Do I need to get up?"

"No, no. I need to get something." She returned to the table a moment later with a mortar and a bag of dried flowers. She opened the bag and dumped the contents into the mortar.

"Potpourri. Just what this reading needed." I sniffed the air between us. Not gonna lie. It smelled good no matter how useless it seemed.

Poco stuck a finger in the mixture and stirred them around. "I was a florist for a reason, smart-ass."

"I thought it was because flowers make everything better."

"And the added bonus that I can use them as scrying materials." She peered at the floral remains. "You're withholding information from me. From everyone."

I resisted the urge to flinch. "What kind of information?"

"I don't know, but whatever it is seems to be affecting

the reading." She peered at me. "If you want this to be accurate, it would help to have all the information."

"I'm not sure what else to tell you," I lied. It was nothing personal; I had to keep my secret. Revealing it to a stranger was a risk not only to me, but my whole crew.

"All right then. Let me focus on this dream of yours. Sorry, nightmare." She sifted through the dried petals. "Your future is bright."

"Well, I did explode like a star. Can't get much brighter than that."

She laughed softly. "I'm not sure about the nightmare, but I'm getting the impression that you're important."

"Isn't everyone important?"

"Nice sentiment. This is different."

"I don't understand."

Poco shrugged. "Maybe that dog you saved is a god in disguise. Maybe there will be someone you rescue in the future who plays a major role in the evolution of our world." She flicked a finger at the mixture. "Who knows? There are forces looking out for you, though. I see multiple shadows around you."

I frowned. "Like the spirits of my ancestors?"

"No, these aren't family members. They aren't..." Her brow furrowed as she studied the petals. "They don't seem to be of this realm." She lifted her head to look at me. "I'm sorry. I don't understand it myself. Maybe the petals are too old. I should toss them."

"No expiration date on the jar, huh?"

Poco's expression remained serious. "There's one more thing I should tell you."

"Should? You mean you don't want to?"

She licked her lips. "I hate being the bearer of bad news, but I suppose it comes with the territory." She released a breath of resignation. "You won't remain hidden forever. Someone close to you will betray you."

I shifted uneasily. "I don't suppose you can give me a hint. Does their name start with the letter 'B?' Even their species might narrow it down."

Poco chuckled softly. "My readings are rarely that specific."

"Even so, it's a good skill to have."

She gazed at the petals. "And that romantic interest I mentioned—please be careful. He's very dangerous."

That ruled nobody out. Everybody I knew was dangerous.

"Quite deadly, too."

Delightful. "I'll be on the lookout for men I'm attracted to that also have a fondness for murder. Shouldn't be too hard to narrow down." In truth, I already had someone in mind, but I couldn't bring myself to acknowledge it out loud. I felt mildly sick to my stomach that he might rise to the level of romantic interest. And here I thought I'd simply experienced a moment of temporary insanity.

"Your companions will have eaten by now. Come, you can break bread with my found family."

"Found family?"

"Those you choose rather than those who are blood relations."

I thought of my crew. Were they my found family or simply my business associates? I honestly wasn't sure.

I followed Poco to another building that housed only a kitchen and a dining area. The long, rectangular table was covered in bowls and plates. I inhaled the aroma of Italian seasoning and nearly fainted from hunger.

A young man with elfin features pulled out the empty chair beside his and gestured for me to sit.

"Thank you," I said, as I scooted the chair closer to the table.

"I'm Gabe," he said.

"Everyone, this is Aster," Poco announced. "She'll be joining us for supper." Poco sat at the head of the table. "Let us pray." She lowered her head and folded her hands on the table.

Gabe groaned. "Do we have to?"

Poco popped one eye open and fixed it on him. "If you want to eat, then yes."

I clasped my hands and listened as Poco thanked the old gods and the new for this bounty and for keeping them safe and healthy.

"I'd like to know what new gods you think there are," Gabe said, once the meal had officially commenced. He passed me a bowl of rice.

"I'm covering my bases," Poco replied smoothly. "If there are any, we'll stay on their good side."

"You're wasting your breath," the girl across from me said. "No one's listening."

Poco gave her a pointed look. "I'm listening."

Scowling, the girl sank deeper into her chair.

"What do you think, Aster?" Gabe asked.

Nothing like being put on the spot. "The food is delicious," I said. I made a show of spooning more gravy over my rice.

"Not about the food. About the existence of gods."

I mulled over the question. "My grandmother used to say that gods are like air. We can't see them or touch them, but neither can we live without them."

Poco smiled. "Wise woman."

"I think we've managed fine without them," Gabe interjected. "We're all sitting here now, aren't we?"

"You didn't tell us *your* opinion," the girl said.

There was one in every crowd. "I can't say I give them much thought."

"Because you're too busy surviving," Gabe shot back. "If the gods cared, they'd ease up on the destruction of civilization and give us a chance to breathe, and maybe make an offering every now and then."

"What's their motive for allowing us to wither and die?" I asked. "If there's no one left to worship them, do they cease to exist?"

"Aha!" Poco jabbed a fork in Gabe's direction. "An excellent question."

"You only think they exist because you've lived a blessed life," Gabe muttered.

Based on my earlier conversation with Poco, I wasn't sure how accurate that was, but it didn't seem like my place to contradict him.

Poco poured water from a pitcher into her cup. "Like I said, I'm hedging my bets. If they're listening, great. If not, no harm done."

Gabe looked at me sideways. "Do you have these kinds of discussions at the dinner table?"

"No," I replied simply. No need to explain that we didn't have a dinner table.

"Gabe and Miriam are contrary no matter what the topic is," a middle-aged woman said. "It's become a sport for them."

"I'm familiar with the type," I commented. No need to name any names, especially when one of them happened to be my traveling companion.

"I heard there's a sickness in your area," the middle-aged woman said. "Is that what brought you to Fairbanks?"

"Yes," I lied.

"Did you find any medicine to treat it?" Gabe asked.

"It seems pretty resistant to medicine," I told him.

Miriam leaned forward with her elbows on the table. "I heard it kills its victims in less than twenty-four hours and turns their bodies inside out."

"It's a disease, not a monster," Gabe corrected her.

"Maybe it's an invisible monster," Miriam replied. "It sounds like they don't know much about it."

"We're working on learning more." That much was true. "We don't want it to spread to other communities. It's a gruesome way to die."

"They're all gruesome if you ask me," the middle-aged woman said. "Give me a peaceful death in my sleep. That's all I ask."

"That can be arranged," Gabe commented.

The woman threw a roll across the table and hit Gabe squarely in the forehead. Everybody laughed, including Gabe. I thought of my grandmother, who would've raked them over the coals for their lack of manners. It didn't bother me, though. In fact, there was something oddly comforting about their behavior. There were a few cantankerous personalities, but they still seemed to genuinely like each other. I wasn't sure I could say the same about our crew. We lived together and worked together, yes, but were we the kind of found family that Poco had described? Did it matter?

After dinner, I carried my empty plate to the kitchen sink where two of the boys were already cleaning the dishes.

Poco joined me in the kitchen. "Your friends are in the hot springs. If you like, Miriam can escort you there."

I wasn't sure that I wanted the unpleasant waif accompanying me, but it seemed rude to refuse. "Sure."

Miriam surprised me by bringing me a change of clothes

before we left. "This way you won't have to worry about waiting for your clothes to dry."

"Thank you." I changed in the bathroom and carried my dry clothes with me in case we didn't return to this building.

Miriam didn't have much to say during our walk. She was more interested in holding the flashlight so that we both could see the path. At least she was considerate.

My three companions cheered when I arrived at the hot springs. Based on the number of empty pint glasses behind them, they seemed like they'd been enjoying more than the warm water.

Bear waved me over. "Join us, Aster."

Even Bonnie appeared to be in a good mood. "This is the most relaxing time I've had in ages." She stuck a toe out of the water and wiggled it.

I unhooked my cloak and draped it on the ground. Then I placed my clothes on top.

Tyson slapped the water. "That's cheating."

"What is?" I asked, dipping a foot into the steaming water.

"We're all naked in here," Tyson replied with a huge grin.

"Yeah, but we spend half our time naked," Bear cut in. "Aster doesn't shift, remember?"

"I'll pass, thanks." I slid the rest of my body into the hot spring and found a flat rock on which to sit. The soothing water more than made up for the discomfort of the seat.

"Can I bring you anything?" Miriam offered.

"Another pitcher," Bear said, waving his empty glass in the air.

"No more," Bonnie cut in. "We have a long journey ahead of us."

"I agree with Bonnie," I said.

Bear booed us both. Tyson wisely remained silent on the subject.

Miriam turned off the flashlight and left it on top of my clothes. She pulled a second one from her pocket and switched it on for the walk back.

"Enjoy yourselves," she called over her shoulder. "Look out for the elk. They sometimes mistake it for a watering hole."

"She's joking, right?" Tyson asked.

"I'd like to see an elk," Bear said.

"Why? So you can punch it in the face?" Tyson laughed at his own joke.

Yep, definitely drunk.

"Any elk with half a brain will run in the opposite direction if it gets a whiff of us," Bonnie said.

I spread my arms behind me and leaned back. "Not me. They like me."

"That's because everybody likes you," Bonnie grumbled. "Our resident golden girl." It didn't exactly sound like a compliment.

Looking at her across the hot springs, I remembered Poco's warning that someone would betray me. My money was on Bonnie, but the question that bothered me most wasn't who.

It was when.

Chapter Twelve

Hugo pounced the moment we set foot in the clearing. "Where's the loot?"

"We had to abort," I said.

Scarlet looked at me askance. "You went all that way and abandoned the mission?"

Bear ambled toward the campfire and liberated a kebab from Hattie's grasp. "It was a setup. We hightailed it out of there before anyone saw us." He swallowed the pieces of the kebab faster than I could register them and tossed the stick on the fire.

"Then why did it take so long to get back?" Hugo asked, with a suspicious glint in his eyes.

"We stopped to see an old friend of mine," Bear said. "May have enjoyed a dip in the hot springs, too."

"How nice for you," Hattie said. "Sounds like a vacation."

Bear seemed to realize he was in hot water that didn't bubble. "It was a really long journey. So much dirt. I'm parched."

His response didn't seem to erase the scowl from her face.

Hugo offered Bear a pouch of water, most likely in an attempt to diffuse the tension. Bear thanked him and took a swig.

"Which old friend was this?" Scarlet asked.

"Poco. I've mentioned her to you before."

She looked at me with a question in her eyes. I didn't answer.

"Any news on the home front?" Tyson asked.

"One of the villages reported a new case but turns out it was just kids playing a prank," Scarlet said.

"Not a very funny one." I was relieved to know it was a prank though.

"They decorated themselves in tiny bits of wet cabbage." Scarlet paused. "You don't want to know how they attempted to recreate the smell."

"You're right. I don't. On that note, I'll be back in a few minutes." I made my way through the trees to the wooden hut that housed our toilet. My bladder was bursting after the long drive because I didn't want to be the one to request a break. The perils of being a team player.

It had been nice to use proper facilities at Aurora Hot Springs. I'd forgotten what it was like to have basic amenities. The outhouse served its purpose, though, so I couldn't complain. We also used a couple waterfalls to shower, and Tyson and Hugo had rigged a rudimentary shower that required the water to be carried rather than pumped. Unfortunately, indoor plumbing was out of the question. Aside from our limited supplies, there was no way we could do the necessary work without drawing attention to the hideout.

By the time I returned to the clearing, Tyson was

regaling everyone with the tale of my river adventure. They clapped as I sat on the end of the log beside Scarlet and she passed me a charred kebab. The black dusting was the best part.

"Exactly how cute was this dog?" Hattie asked.

"Billy was the only connection that woman had left to the world," I said. If the dog had died, I had no doubt the woman would've hurled herself into the river.

Hattie giggled. "Who names a dog Billy?"

"I suspect it was in honor of someone," I said.

"That dog must be part cat because it definitely should be dead, if not from the monster than the number of times it was underwater," Hugo remarked.

"It felt longer than it actually was," I said. In my experience, everything seems to happen in slow motion during a crisis.

Hugo snagged my gaze. "Tyson said the monster you fought wore a jeweled crown."

I smiled. "Not quite. It was a crystal embedded in its forehead, according to a reliable source."

Bonnie chewed with her mouth open. "Since when do monsters have naturally occurring jewelry?"

"I bet that crystal is worth a fortune," Hugo said.

I held up a hand. "Don't even think about it. Those creatures are rare and deadly. It was a miracle that we encountered one at all."

"And lived to tell us about it," Scarlet added. "I'm sorry the trip was a bust."

"It's my fault. I should've realized we were being played."

Hugo cast a speculative glance at me. "Why didn't you?"

I kept my attention on the kebab. Food was more

appealing than Hugo any day of the week. "I was focused on the investigation and the fact that Lord Doran himself was asking for my cooperation."

"And you believed him?" Hugo shook his head in dismay.

"His reasoning made sense to me." That much was true.

"Do you think he really lost three vampires to the Green Death?" Hattie asked. "If he lied, that could mess with the investigation."

She made a good point. I'd exclude it for now and only focus on the humans.

"What's on the agenda for tomorrow then?" Scarlet asked.

"I'd like to go to Berthold and check on any developments."

Bear's hand shot up. "I volunteer."

Bonnie elbowed him. "You only want to go to the pub."

"Why can't I want to do both?" Bear washed his third kebab down with more water.

"You had enough beer at the hot springs to last a week," Bonnie said.

"I'll take Scarlet and Hattie," I announced.

"Scarlet's your number two," Hugo said. "Is it wise to travel so far together?"

"Once in a blue moon isn't going to be the end of the world," Scarlet replied.

"It is when there's a plague spreading through The Wild," Hugo shot back.

"Would you like to join our party, Hugo?" I asked, already knowing the answer.

His lips parted in a faint smile. "I think that's a splendid idea."

"Fine, I'll stay here like I always do." Scarlet stabbed a kebab stick at the flames.

"But you do it so well," Hugo said in a smug tone.

"I believe you've got outhouse duty tomorrow," Scarlet reminded him. "Make sure you take care of that before you leave."

I sensed a fight brewing. I was too tired from the journey to deal with it, so I stretched and yawned. "I'll see everybody tomorrow."

A chorus of voices urged me to "sleep well" as I climbed to my tree house. My blanket was folded neatly on the floor. I shook it out and wrapped it around my body until I felt like I was in a cocoon. When I closed my eyes, a vision of Lord Doran appeared in my mind. His broad shoulders. Those eyes that seemed to reflect my magic.

I shoved the memory aside and tried to think about something else, refusing to linger over my attraction to the ruthless vampire. I should be furious with him for playing me and I was worried about someone's impending betrayal. I reminded myself that Lord Doran was responsible for the purge, among other terrible events. He was ruthless and deadly, and he wanted me dead. Or at least he wanted the Hooded One dead. There. That helped.

I turned on my side and listened to the chatter below. There was no hostility in their voices now. Soft laughter drifted to my ears. Crisis averted. I remembered the lively conversation over dinner at Aurora Hot Springs and longed for that kind of dynamic. Miriam and Gabe could snipe at each other, but at the end of the day, they still considered each other family. My crew could snipe at each other, but I wasn't convinced we all had each other's backs the way we pretended. The realization was unsettling. I'd fooled myself into believing we were loyal to each other, in part because no one had revealed my identity, but also because there were no other options. I'd been desperate after the death of my family and the dispersion of the coven. Eventually, I'd assembled a replacement group for the sake of my survival. On occasion we'd lose a member like we did with Victor, but mostly we pressed on —together.

I tossed and turned, wanting to sleep but not wanting to dream. My mind knew this was an unreasonable request and that resistance was futile. I could no more control my dreams than I could control the world around me. Finally, my breathing grew steady, and I slipped into slumber.

I awoke to the smell of smoke drifting through the tree house and hurried to the crow's nest to investigate. I was surprised to see the smoke was blowing from Klondike.

I fled the tree house and made a beeline through the forest, nearly colliding with Hugo.

' "You saw it?" he asked.

"Hard to miss it. What's happening?"

"The blood bank burned to the ground."

"Arson?"

Hugo hesitated. "You won't like the answer."

"What do you mean?"

"I heard vampires claim to have seen the Hooded One fleeing the scene."

My stomach sank. If vampires were going to start hunting me again, I'd have to lay low, which meant hitting the pause button on my investigation of the Green Death.

"Sorry," he said. "I didn't want to have to be the one to tell you."

"It's okay. Better that I know." I didn't like being sidelined at the best of times, but now was particularly challeng-ing. "Was anybody inside?"

"Not sure. It's outside of their regular hours, so I doubt it."

"Let's hope." I couldn't imagine showing up to 'donate' and then being further traumatized by a fire.

"We should get you away from here."

I tore my gaze from the smoke. "I'm planning to head back now."

"Not the hideout. Somewhere else."

I laughed. "Where else would I go?"

"I know the others won't say anything because it's you, but your continued presence puts us all in danger."

"That's nothing new. I'm the Hooded One, remember?"

"I know, but thanks to this blaze, the heat will be on." He paused. "No pun intended."

"Where do you suggest I go? It isn't as though we have hideouts from our hideout." The Wild was exactly as the name suggested.

"What about one of the outer villages like Clayton? At least until the response to this dies down."

I bristled at the suggestion. "There hasn't even *been* a response yet."

Hugo compressed his lips. "Come on, Aster. You're smarter than this. We get ahead of them. We don't wait for them to make a move. That's how we've survived all these years."

Engines roared to life. Hugo and I knew better than to continue our disagreement when Beasts were on their way. We turned and ran, opting for a path where the trees were too dense for Beasts to pass through.

"Did you notice them?" he asked once the sound of Beasts had dissipated.

"The tracks? Yeah." We'd passed dozens of wolf prints between the donation center and here.

"Should we go back and examine them?"

"You don't think they belong to our crew?"

He grunted. "Did you see the size of the one pair? Even Tyson doesn't have paws that large. Not even close."

I cast a glance over my shoulder. "Do you think we should be concerned?"

Hugo shrugged. "Maybe we have them to thank for the fire."

"I don't think we should thank anybody for that. It only makes life more difficult."

"For you, you mean."

"For all of us. Just because they blame me doesn't mean I'm the one who'll suffer their retaliation." I shuddered in response to my own statement. There would be a price to pay for this, and I wasn't looking forward to finding out the cost.

By the time we returned to the hideout, the rest of the crew was gathered around the campfire.

"Maybe we should put that out for now," Hugo suggested. "The woods will be crawling with rangers."

"Good idea." Bear set to work dousing the flames.

"Hugo thinks I should lay low in Clayton."

Scarlet shot to her feet. "Absolutely not. We need you here."

"And the odds of getting to keep her here increase if she goes to Clayton today," Hugo said in a reasonable voice.

"I agree with Hugo," Bonnie said. She shot me an apologetic look. "Not that I want to get rid of you, Aster, but if rangers are hunting for you, it's best if they don't find you."

"They don't know who I am," I reminded them. "If they're hunting for me, they could come here regardless of whether I'm physically present. Even worse, they might mistake one of you for me."

Hattie raised a hand. "Can I say something?"

"Go ahead," Hugo told her.

"I don't think we should separate. If Aster goes to Clayton, we should all go."

"Why do you think that?" Hugo pressed.

"Because, like she said, the rangers won't know who they're looking for. If they find us and she isn't here, they might still decide one of us is the Hooded One."

"And she won't be here to protect us," Scarlet added.

"Are you serious with that shit?" Tyson interrupted. "We don't need Aster to protect us. We're all more than capable of handling ourselves in a fight with rangers or any other vampire."

"Settle down, Tyson's ego," Scarlet said sharply. "No one's trying to insult you."

The larger werewolf stood upright, expanding his chest in the process. "Takes more than that to bruise my ego. I'm merely pointing out that your concerns are unfounded."

"I think if we all would have to go to Clayton, then we all might as well stay right here," Hattie said. "They haven't managed to find us yet, and they've looked plenty of times before."

I rubbed my hands in front of the fire to keep warm. "I agree with Hattie."

"Let's put it to a vote," Scarlet said. "All in favor of Aster staying put, raise your hand."

Everybody raised a hand except Bonnie and Hugo.

"That settles it." I dusted off my hands.

"What are you doing?" Hugo asked.

"What I intended to do earlier before I got sidetracked by the fire. Continue my research on the Green Death."

He grabbed my arm. "You can't be serious. Give it a day, at the very least."

I looked at Scarlet, who nodded. "Fine, I'll hang here for today, but I don't have to act happy about it."

Bonnie slapped me on the back. "Very mature."

"There's something else," I said. "Hugo and I saw wolf prints between here and Klondike."

"Big deal," Bonnie said. "We travel that route all the time."

"They don't belong to any of you," Hugo interjected.

Hattie bounced on her seat. "Ghost Pack. I told you!"

Hugo frowned. "Now that you mention it, there was one set of prints that was larger than all the others."

Bear whistled. "The White Wolf right here in our little neck of the woods?"

I shot him a quizzical look. "Who's that?"

"You've never heard of the White Wolf?" Tyson asked in awe.

"She's not one of us," Bonnie snapped. "Why would she know?"

I let her comment roll off my back.

"The White Wolf is the alpha of the Ghost Pack," Bear explained. "He's like a mythical figure. Larger than life. Rips vampires to shreds like they're made of paper."

I was unimpressed by his description. "Great. More violence. Just what we need here."

"If the Ghost Pack is here, how have we not seen them or smelled them?" Scarlet asked.

Bear grinned. "It's right there in the name. Ghost Pack."

"But they're not actually ghosts," Scarlet replied.

Bear cocked an eyebrow. "Aren't they? We don't know anything for certain."

I tossed a stick on the fire. "We know ghosts don't leave paw prints."

"Fair enough," Bear said. "Maybe we should form a search party. See what they want."

"Maybe they want to be more of a nuisance to the vampires than we've managed to be," Hugo remarked.

"If they're the ones who torched the blood bank, then they're already ahead of us," Bonnie said.

My whole body tensed. "If they're the ones who did it, then they're going to have a problem with me."

Tyson looked up at me from a seated position. "One meeting with Lord Doran and you're a vampire supporter?"

"I don't have to be a vampire supporter to see that arson is wrong. Innocent people could've died." In fact, innocent people *would* die once word reached Lords Birney and Doran. There was no chance they'd let such a destructive act go without a response.

"You're a real hypocrite, you know that?" Bonnie said.

I ignored her and headed into the woods. If I couldn't leave, I could at least take out my frustration with target practice.

Hattie joined me a few minutes later. Most of the wolves turned their noses up at archery, but Hattie was keen to learn. I bet if she had the ability to conjure spells, she would've been thrilled to learn those too. She was our resident sponge, albeit with temperamental hormones. I'd been different at her age. I hadn't given romantic relationships any thought. To be fair, I didn't give them any thought now either. The stakes seemed perpetually high, and there was simply no room for anything that resembled a 'normal' life.

"Clayton is a dump," Hattie remarked as she released

another arrow, narrowly missing the target. "I'm glad we didn't have to go there."

"As opposed to our luxury headquarters," I said with a laugh. "At least Clayton has indoor plumbing."

A wolf barreled into the clearing and nearly collided with us. The fur and claws retracted to reveal Bear.

"What the hell?" Hattie demanded.

Panting, Bear twisted his head to look at us. "Rangers."

My pulse raced. "Here?"

He shook his head. "Villages."

The earth seemed to stand still. It seemed that Doran's retaliation for the destruction of the blood bank was swift and immediate. Rangers had descended upon the villages and dragged able-bodied young men and women from their homes. Aside from their youth, there didn't seem to be specific criteria. The message was clear, though. Screw with me again, and I'll wipe out your next generation.

Everybody except Hattie headed to Berthold. I didn't want her to witness any of the aftermath. I knew the kind of nightmares that would haunt her if she did.

A small crowd approached us on our way to the village.

A man grabbed my sleeve. "You're her. You're the Hooded One."

Instinctively, I jerked my arm out of his reach.

The man stared at me with wild eyes. "Rangers attacked us. They dragged people into the square and executed them."

"At random?"

"They took my son," the woman behind him cried. "My Adam. He was only twenty-two."

This was exactly what I feared would happen.

Another man approached us. "We can't let them treat us like lambs at the slaughter. We need to fight back."

"Violence begets violence, James," an older woman said. "If you attack them, you're no better than they are. You're just continuing the cycle."

James whirled to face her. "So we let them use us as food and then murder us at will?"

"Please calm down," I said in a loud voice.

Adam's mother moved to stand directly in my path. "You can kill them, can't you? Why not go right now and murder those rangers that killed my son?"

"Yes, do it," James insisted. "What's the good of having powerful magic if you don't use it to defend us?"

"That isn't defending us," the older woman said. "That's revenge, attacking them the same as they attacked us."

"I'd suggest you all find a safe place to stay until this blows over. If you have friends in Oglethorpe or Clayton or another village, see if they can put you up."

The older woman cut through the cluster of bodies. "What about you?"

"I'm going to see their handiwork." I needed to see first-hand what the rangers had done.

"Bring me something from my Adam, please," his mother begged, tugging my sleeve. "He's wearing a silver band that belonged to my father. Bring me that. I can't look."

"I'll do my best," I told her. My response seemed to placate her because she released my cloak and merged with the crowd.

My stomach became increasingly unsettled the closer I got to the square. There was no sign of fire, which meant they didn't burn the bodies. It made sense. They wanted to make an example of these people. Better to leave their rotting corpses in plain sight in the middle of the village square.

Sure enough, I arrived in the square to find seven bodies tied to seven posts. There was no one else in view. No vampires. No villagers. The victims had been drained of blood—waste not, want not, apparently.

A tightness spread across my chest as I observed them. Memories cut through my thoughts. Tearful coven members. Witches and wizards searching for those missing. I'd discovered the limp body of my cat, Willow, beneath a splintered piece of wood. It appeared she'd been trampled. I'd buried her myself. I couldn't bring myself to burn the body even though I knew that's what I was supposed to do. The others had been too preoccupied to notice. Grief and panic were the primary emotions at the time.

"Aster, did you hear me?"

I returned to the present and tried to focus. "Sorry, what?" I wasn't even sure who'd spoken to me.

"We should help them with the bodies," Bear said.

"Yes, of course." I moved on autopilot and tried to disconnect from reality. I didn't want to register the girl's small hands. Someone said she was sixteen, but she was so petite, she could easily have been mistaken for a younger child. I wondered whether the vampires knew her real age or simply didn't care. Sixteen or six. What did it really matter? An innocent child had been murdered by the authorities.

I steeled myself as I approached the first body. He looked to have been around thirty years old. I checked his fingers for a ring, but they were bare.

I retrieved a small knife from my boot and began to cut down the victims. I didn't want the bodies to be here when the villagers returned. It would ignite hatred and violence all over again.

It occurred to me that the party responsible for burning down the donation center may have wanted this outcome. If people were upset enough, maybe they'd revolt, like the ones threatening violence in the woods. I hated to break it to them, but there were no winners in a situation like this. My sun-kissed magic wasn't a solution either. Even if I wiped out every vampire in The Wild, which was unlikely, there was a whole world full of them. And they weren't all rangers willing to execute innocent people. Some vampires were proponents of synthetic blood and supported the humane treatment of people. We couldn't paint them all with the same brush.

I glanced at Bear and Tyson as they took down the other bodies and lowered them to the ground. I couldn't believe Lord Doran would stoop to this level.

What was I thinking? Of course I could. He'd done it to my coven. Yet it was hard to reconcile these actions with the vampire I'd met. He was bristly and authoritative, but I didn't sense the brutality and ruthlessness that I expected.

And everyone would believe the Hooded One was responsible. They'd blame me, which increased the risk that someone would turn me in. I remembered Poco's prediction of a betrayal, and a shiver racked my body. It took a village to defend me, but it would only take one person to destroy me.

Chapter Thirteen

I let a couple days pass before I ventured back to the village. I wore a black cloak and tied my auburn hair in a ponytail to keep from being recognized. I wasn't sure what the general feeling was toward me at the moment, but I didn't want to let fear and guilt prevent me from making progress on the Green Death. Despite offers to accompany me, I thought it best to travel alone.

Frank and Mauve sat at a table at the back of the Dancing Dragon. Because they were from the villages affected by the Green Death, I'd requested the two healers meet with me. I was hoping to work together to pinpoint the cause.

Frank was a wiry man with tufts of gray hair sprouting from his otherwise bald head. His gaunt face was covered in creases and his jowls were saggy, which seemed more a product of excessive vices than age.

The moment I spotted the empty pitcher in front of Frank, I realized I'd made a mistake asking them to meet at the pub.

"Sorry I'm late," I said, joining them at the round table.

"Did anyone give you a hard time?" Mauve asked.

I shook my head.

"You didn't have anything to do with the blood bank, did you?" Frank asked.

"Of course not," Mauve answered for me. "Aster would never do a thing like that."

Frank belched. "Whoever did it had to know the vampires would take it out on us, especially with Lord Birney in the area."

Mauve played with her cutlery. "It won't stop them from setting up a temporary place until the donation center can be rebuilt."

"Who would be stupid enough to taunt the Fallen? We know what they're capable of." Frank hunched forward and pinned his gaze on me. "And you know better than most."

I recoiled slightly, catching a whiff of beer-soaked breath. "I'm not here to talk about the donation center. I want your help with stopping the Green Death before it kills the whole community."

Frank responded to that by signaling for another pitcher of beer. Great.

Meredith hustled to the table with a full pitcher. "Aster, I didn't notice you come in. What can I get for you?"

"An empty glass for the beer is fine."

"Mom tested a new recipe for vegetable stew. I have to say, I think it's a winner." She watched me expectantly.

"Okay, twist my arm."

Meredith broke into a smile. "You won't regret it. I know you think there's only so many ways to make vegetables interesting, but when you're as creative as my mom, the sky's the limit." She set the pitcher in the center of the table and returned to the kitchen.

Frank immediately reached for the pitcher, but Mauve slapped his hand away. "Give it a rest, Frank."

Frank cleared his throat and focused on me. "How do you think we can help?"

I dipped a hand into my cloak pocket and withdrew a folded map. I spread it open across the table. "I thought if we can identify victims' locations on a map, that might help us pinpoint commonalities."

Frank observed the map. "This isn't accurate. It's missing a few roads in this village."

"It was probably made before the roads had names," Mauve snapped. The witch had clearly already had enough of Frank prior to my arrival.

"I guess that's true. The Wild is always changing. That's the one constant."

"Same could be said for the world, not just here," Mauve replied. "Vampires think they're gods on earth now, but give it time. Eventually they'll fall off the top of the food chain the same way humans did. Power is cyclical, just like life itself."

Frank stared at her through slitted eyes. "Have you always sounded this wise or am I just drunk?"

Mauve ignored him. "You should've just invited me. This one's useless."

Meredith sailed back to our table and set a plate and glass in front of me. If the stew tasted half as good as it smelled, I was in for a treat.

"Thank you. Tell Rita I appreciate her experiments."

"Anything else for you?" Meredith's gaze skimmed right past Frank.

"Do you have a pen or a marker?" I asked.

Meredith rooted through her apron and produced a thin black marker. "Will this do?"

"Perfect." I plucked the marker from her and set it on the map.

Meredith angled her head toward the table. "What's the map for?"

"A public health crisis." Mauve uncapped the marker and put a dot in the area marked Whitehead. "This is where one of the victims lived." She added a second dot. "This is where he worked."

Meredith leaned over to examine the map. "You're searching for a pattern?"

"Anything that might point to a source," I said. "A pattern. Commonalities."

Mauve marked a few more places in Whitehead and set down the marker. Frank snatched it from the table and added a dot in Berthold. I tried to focus on the map, but the stew was so delicious that I had a hard time concentrating on anything else. I should've waited to eat until after the meeting.

"I don't know which spices your mom used, but compliments to the chef," I said.

Meredith beamed. "Oh, I can't wait to tell her. She'll be so pleased."

I filled my glass with beer from the pitcher. "Do you have anything to add to our map, Meredith?"

She chewed her lip as she contemplated the existing marks. "You missed Oglethorpe."

Mauve and I exchanged frowns. "Someone died of the Green Death in Oglethorpe?" I asked.

Meredith nodded. "Two someones. That's what I heard anyway. Maybe it's only a rumor."

I marked two dots in Oglethorpe, which was northeast of Whitehead.

"That's disturbing," Mauve said. "It suggests the disease

is spreading."

"Have any patients come to you with symptoms that could be the start of the Green Death?" I asked.

They shook their heads in unison.

"Even if they did, I wouldn't know what to treat them with," Mauve admitted. "I have tonics for a fever, but nothing for those terrible sores."

An idea occurred to me. "Ingrid from the Lunar Cafe is growing a plant called anemone nemorosa. She said it has healing properties. Could that help?"

Mauve grunted. "That's debatable."

"You don't use it for healing?"

"Windflower? Absolutely not. I told her she was wasting her time growing it, but you know there's always a bit of tension between earth witches and healers like me."

"She said she sells it to healers."

"Maybe she does, but I'm not one of them."

Their disagreement might explain Ingrid's reaction when I mentioned Mauve's name.

"You know what? It doesn't matter anyway. Her wind-flower went missing a couple weeks ago, along with the ginger plants."

"Unfortunately, you're not the only thief in The Wild, Aster, though I suspect it was an opportunistic theft."

"Nobody with actual plant knowledge would take windflower," Frank blurted.

I looked at the drunken healer. "Why not?"

"Because anemone nemorosa was once believed to be the origin of all diseases. If people saw the flowers in bloom in the wild, they'd hold their breath. They thought the surrounding air was contaminated by death."

The three of us stared at each other.

"That settles it," Frank said. "This disease has to be

airborne. We need to continue to tell anyone looking after the sick to take precautions."

Despite a strong desire to savor the stew, I shoveled down the remainder of it so I could focus on the meeting. "Let's not jump to conclusions."

"It's not jumping," Frank argued. "Oglethorpe is miles away."

Mauve swiveled in her seat to address him. "And what? You think a stiff breeze delivered the Green Death to their doorsteps and no one else's?"

I studied Frank. "Do you think it's a coincidence that a plant with that reputation is missing?"

Mauve frowned. "Are you suggesting someone stole windflower from Ingrid's cafe and is now killing people with it?"

"Could be accidental," Frank said. "Either way, that plant is bad news. In China, they called it the Flower of Death. In Egypt, it was considered the embodiment of sickness."

"Why would Ingrid grow a plant like that?" I asked, more to myself.

"Ignorance," Frank replied. "That's the trouble with breaking up a coven. You get practitioners messing with things they shouldn't."

"I don't think windflower is responsible, at least not randomly," Mauve said. "It's folklore. I don't use it because it doesn't have the effective healing properties some people claim."

I looked at Meredith. "What do we know about the victims in Oglethorpe?"

"Two women is all I know."

"They might've visited the shops in Whitehead or

Berthold in the past week," Mauve pointed out. "Stopped for a bite to eat."

"Still doesn't rule out airborne," Frank said.

"I've already ruled out a food source," I told them. "None of the victims had any meals in common."

"What if it's an ingredient, though?" Meredith asked. "Mom uses the same herbs and spices in multiple dishes, but nobody would necessarily know what they are."

Mauve nodded. "That's an excellent point."

"Maybe somebody used that plant as an ingredient, not realizing it could hurt people?" Meredith suggested.

"How are we supposed to determine that?" Frank asked. "It's impossible to figure out every ingredient in every single meal the victims ate in the day or so leading up to their deaths."

"Difficult but not impossible," Mauve clarified.

"Excuse me," a voice interrupted. "Is it possible to order food at the bar?"

Meredith spun around to answer him. Given his size, I couldn't believe none of us noticed him until he spoke. He was easily six-and-a-half feet tall with white-blond hair and a body of corded muscle. His eyes were an unnatural color, like two blue diamonds, clear and sharp and devastatingly beautiful. There was something vaguely familiar about him.

"Yes, of course," Meredith sputtered. "Anything you want."

Appearing to sense my attention, his gaze slid to me. "Looks like you've got quite an operation going. Planning a heist?"

Frank practically guffawed.

"Trying to prevent another plague," I replied.

"Are you new to the village?" Mauve asked. "I haven't seen you before."

The implication was clear—this guy would be impossible to miss, except all four of us had done exactly that until he interrupted us.

"I'm passing through, although sometimes if I see something I like, I might hang around for a bit. See how things pan out." He kept his eyes locked on mine, and a tiny shiver rippled through me.

"An adventurer," Frank said approvingly. "I like your spirit, young man."

"Max," he said. "My name is Max."

It was hard to tell exactly how old Max was. Despite his youthful appearance, his eyes seemed to reflect decades of experiences, and not all of them good.

"If you take a seat at the bar, I can bring you a menu," Meredith said.

"A pleasure to meet you, Max," Mauve said.

"Likewise." He grinned at me. "See you around."

I noticed Mauve checking out his butt as he walked away. Meredith fanned herself before scurrying to the stack of menus.

I set aside any thoughts of Max and his impressive backside and focused on the matter at hand.

"I think we need more information about these women," I said. "I'll travel to Oglethorpe and see what I can find out."

Mauve gazed at the map. "I think Whitehead has to be the source, but I can't quite put my finger on it yet."

Frank waved a dismissive hand. "How can you say that when you had a case right here in Berthold and two in Oglethorpe?"

"Because the victim in Berthold worked in Whitehead," Mauve said simply. "Which means he spent most of his time there."

"What about Oglethorpe?" Frank pressed. "You think

these two women also worked in Whitehead? I'd be surprised if that was the case." He smacked the map. "Airborne, I tell you. Those noxious odors carry the disease to the victim's lungs and infect the body."

"I think if that were true, we'd see a lot more people dying," Mauve countered.

"Setting aside this new information," I interjected, "are there any common factors between the victims we already know about?"

The three of us studied the map in vain.

"Those women may not have died from the Green Death," Mauve said. "There was already a hoax case with those children."

I downed my beer. "I don't know. It's hard to misdiagnose the cause of death with those symptoms."

I checked the time. If I didn't leave now, it would be too late to go to Oglethorpe. I didn't want to leave it until tomorrow.

"I need to go. I appreciate you meeting me."

"Let me know what you find out," Mauve said.

"Let *us* know," Frank added. "If we need to put out a public health alert, we should do it sooner rather than later."

Mauve snorted. "Who needs an alert? Most of The Wild has already heard of the Green Death."

"Yes, but we need to get the details right, so we don't set off a mass panic."

Finally, a sensible point from Frank. His drunken sleepiness seemed to have passed.

"People aren't worried about getting sick anymore," Mauve said. "They're worried about getting executed."

I left money on the table. "If you hear of any more victims, send me a message."

"Take care of yourself, Aster," Mauve said. "There's a target on your back now."

"There's been a target on my back since the purge," I called over my shoulder.

The stool where Max had been seated was now empty. I hadn't noticed him leave. Then again, I'd been preoccupied.

I waved to Meredith on my way out and started toward the Beast's hiding spot. My heartbeat intensified when I spotted a figure in the passenger seat. At first glance I thought it was a ranger trying to reclaim it. Then I noticed the shock of white-blond hair.

"What do you think you're doing?" I demanded, appearing alongside him.

Max looked up at me, wearing an expression of pure innocence. "Oh, is this yours? I thought it might've been abandoned."

"I covered it in branches to keep it hidden so nobody would steal it."

He grinned. "Congratulations. It worked. I haven't stolen it."

I folded my arms. "And now you may exit the vehicle."

"I told you my name, but you didn't tell me yours."

"You're just realizing that now?"

His grin widened. "You should know, I'm a big fan of sassy women. Huge turn-on." He glanced at his crotch. "And I do mean huge."

A real charmer. "Get out of my vehicle, Max."

He vaulted over the side and landed directly beside me, forcing me to take a step backward. I knew he was tall, but having him so close to me brought the reality home. I was five-foot-eight, which was on the taller end of the spectrum for women, but Max had to be part giant. His scent was a combination of mint and beer. I pushed the thought aside. Good grief. What did I care about his scent? Clearly, I'd been spending too much time in the company of werewolves.

"Were those your prints I saw outside Klondike?" I asked.

"Could be. I've been touring the area."

"With a pack?"

"Can't be an alpha without a pack now, can I?"

"Did you have something to do with the fire at the donation center?"

His smile evaporated. "Why would you think that?"

"Because your pack's prints suggested you were fleeing the scene."

Up close, his eyes were even more mesmerizing. I tore my gaze away and tried to focus on other body parts.

Bad idea.

I looked past him at the Beast instead.

"I don't like vampires, but we're not in the business of hurting innocent people, which that arson job most certainly did."

We agreed on that point.

"I'd like some personal space," I said.

"You're free to move."

"You launched yourself into my space. I think you should move."

His grin returned. "Did I mention I also like stubborn women who suffer from overconfidence?"

"Where's your pack now? Shouldn't you be leading them in a howling session or something?"

"Like you, I need my space." He made a show of stepping backward to put distance between us.

"Have we met before? You seem familiar."

"I think you'd remember if we had. I don't exactly blend."

Then it hit me. "Fairbanks. That's where I saw you. At the Golden Heart Plaza." He'd worn a blue skull cap at the time, which is why I didn't recognize his hair. "Have you been following me?"

"My pack has traveled all over the Outer Territories. It's no surprise that we might've crossed paths before."

I narrowed my eyes at him. "That's not an answer." I cocked my head. "You were waiting for me out here. Why?"

"Because I wanted to meet you."

"You met me inside."

"Not properly."

I couldn't decide whether I was flattered or pissed off. "Do you work for Lord Doran?"

My question garnered a chuckle. "Not in a million years. Why would he be sending someone to follow you?"

Ignoring his question, I climbed into the driver's seat and fired up the Beast. "Fair warning. Next time you follow me, you'll find an arrow at your head."

He leaned over the passenger door. "Fair warning. Next time I follow you, you'll be happy I did."

"Ha! Doubtful." I hit the gas, forcing Max to jump backward. I didn't bother to glance behind me. I knew he was still there, watching me go. What I didn't know was why.

Chapter Fourteen

T he village of Oglethorpe didn't really have a
central point like its neighbors. There was no
square or main drag. No overarching influence
like the Bavarian buildings in Berthold. Houses and stores
seemed to have been dropped from the heavens and stayed
where they landed. Higgledy piggledy as my grandmother
used to call it.

Olive McMurtry was the proud owner of Olive Branch,
a used bookstore and cafe. Unlike many of the other cafe
owners in the area, Olive was human. Her parents moved
from Juneau to The Wild when she was a teenager. She
once described her reaction to the area as love at first sight.

"Hey, Olive." I skimmed the titles of a row of books on a
table by the door.

"Aster, how great to see you." Olive was solidly built—
like a well-crafted armoire she liked to tell people—and had
the kind of catlike eyes that I previously thought only
existed in drawings. Cosmetics weren't widely popular in
The Wild, but that didn't stop Olive from accentuating her

positives. She lined her unusual eyes with a charcoal pencil, shaded her eyelids, and lengthened her lashes as far as they were willing to go. The only thing she liked more than a smoky eye was a good book.

Her cat, Nike, was curled on top of a bookshelf. She raised her head, her eyes still in slits from sleepiness, and immediately lowered it again. I was neither a threat nor a favorite. I had to admit, I appreciated being left alone.

"Hattie was in here recently. She bought a book on demons." Olive grimaced. "I hope it isn't keeping her awake."

"I think reality is more of a factor at the moment."

Olive's expression grew pained. "I heard what happened in Berthold. Such a tragedy."

I nodded. "Have you heard any details about the donation center?"

"Only that you were spotted fleeing the scene, but we all know that isn't true. Part of me wonders if the vampires burned down their own building just to have an excuse to kill people and lay the blame at your feet."

I'd considered that possibility, too.

Olive dropped her voice. "Did you hear we've been hit with the Green Death?"

"That's the reason I'm here, actually. I was hoping you could tell me the names of the victims."

"Sure can. Lois Bridges and her daughter, Leesa. So sad. They've only lived here a couple years, but everybody liked them. Lois was known for her knitting, and Leesa played cards with the Gin Rummy Honeys."

"Can you tell me where they lived?"

"Make a right out of here, a left on Spruce, and then a right on Evergreen. Number 11. Her nephew, Landon, is there now to clear out the place."

"He didn't wait long."

Olive shrugged. "I don't blame him. He figures people will be able to use what they had. No sense leaving things to sit around collecting dust."

Fair point. Upon reflection, I would do the same.

A board book caught my gaze. Its sturdy pages were clearly designed for the destructive hands of toddlers. It looked to be about a ladybug.

Olive noticed the object of my attention. "Anything I should know?"

I laughed awkwardly. "No, not me. A friend."

"It's a brave woman who's willing to rear a child in this world."

I couldn't decide whether it was courage, hubris, or stubborn optimism.

"I'll let you have it half price. How about that?"

My eyebrows lifted. "Are you sure?"

"For you? Honestly, I should probably let you have it for free, but I'm too cheap."

We both laughed.

"That Hattie is a bright spark. She said she left school when she was nine."

I nodded. "Wasn't by choice."

"Didn't think so." Olive stroked the cat, who had migrated over to the counter during our conversation. "Do you think she'd be interested in part-time work?"

"Here?"

"Yes." Olive cocked her head. "Do you think Oglethorpe is too far for her to travel on her own every day?"

It wasn't convenient. Realistically, Hattie would need to move to the village.

"Did you broach the subject with her when she was here?"

"No, I didn't want to overstep. I know she doesn't have any family ... I figured you were the closest she has to kin."

"I'll float the idea past her."

Nike rolled over to encourage Olive to rub her belly. Olive's fingers immediately disappeared in the cat's thick fur.

"I have a spare room at my house," Olive said. "I'd been saving it for my niece, but she's decided to stay in Juneau."

"Has she been here before?"

Olive shifted her focus to the cat. "She visited a month or so ago and decided The Wild isn't for her. She prefers city life."

I shuddered, prompting a laugh from Olive.

"My feelings exactly," she said. "The upside is, though, that now I have a part-time position available, as well as room and board."

As much as I hated to lose a member of our crew, especially in light of Victor's death, a move like this would be good for Hattie. The life of an outlaw wasn't for everyone, and Hattie was so young. Olive's offer would give the werewolf a chance to live as close to a normal life as possible. She should do it for the indoor plumbing alone.

"I'll definitely let her know. Thanks for thinking of her."

She inclined her head toward the ladybug book. "Let me know if you want me to set that aside for you."

"Thank you. I'll consider it." A book seemed premature, unless Bonnie wanted to read to her stomach. Did parents-to-be do that? I had no idea.

A memory flashed in my mind of my father sitting on the edge of my bed reading from a book. I couldn't remember the title. There was a toad. He seemed fancy.

I didn't think about my father very often. Sometimes it was easier to pretend I didn't have a past. That way I didn't have to dwell on uncomfortable feelings. They were all gone now—mother, father, grandmother, cousins. I was alone.

"I'll see you next time, Olive." I rubbed Nike's head before turning to exit the building. There was something calming about Olive Branch. Hattie would be lucky to make a home here.

I followed the instructions Olive had given me and made my way to Lois and Leesa's house. The roads weren't straightforward. They were as random and unexpected as the placement of the buildings.

The front door stood open when I arrived. "Hello?" I called. "Landon?"

A rubber dinosaur head popped up from behind the kitchen counter. I had an arrow aimed at his head before he could make a sound.

Two human arms blocked the dinosaur mask. "Sorry, it's not a real T-Rex."

Exhaling, I lowered my bow. "I didn't think you were, but I was still taken aback."

"Can I help you?" the muffled voice asked.

"My name is Aster. I'm looking into the Green Death and was hoping to ask you a few questions about your aunt and cousin."

He stood in silence for a brief moment. "It was so unexpected."

"I know. I'm sorry for your loss."

"You think the people you care about are going to live forever, which is so stupid considering the mortality rate in The Wild," the T-Rex continued. "Somehow you think everyone you know is immune."

"You're sure it was the Green Death?"

The T-Rex nodded. "Started with a fever. Then green pus leaking out of sores on their skin and the worst smell you could imagine. Does that sound right?"

"Yes, it does."

"Why don't we talk outside so I can take off this mask? My head needs a break anyway."

We moved outside the house and slowly he peeled off the dinosaur mask. His face was covered in sweat.

"Nice mask, by the way."

"I had this from a Halloween party a few years ago. It was the best I could do." He extended a hand. "I'm Landon."

I shook his hand, which was less sweaty than his head. I hadn't seen anyone celebrate Halloween since I was a little girl. The coven celebrated Samhain, of course, but it had felt strange to honor a sky we couldn't see.

"If you're looking into the Green Death, why don't you have some kind of face protection?" he asked.

"I've been investigating it since it started. If you could breathe it in, we'd all be extinct by now." Despite Frank's insistence and the description of the missing plant, the evidence still suggested the sickness wasn't transmitted by air.

"If the disease isn't airborne, then how did they catch it?" Landon asked.

"I believe it's something they ingested. Their bodies were burned?"

His mouth tightened. "Yes, ma'am. I lit the torch myself. Hope I never have to do anything like that again."

"It's hard. I know."

"The stench was the worst part, I think. I've left the door open twenty-four seven to try to air out the house. I only closed it earlier today when I saw an elk wander past the house. I didn't want him to think he had an open invitation."

"I don't see too many elk anymore."

"Me neither. Aunt Lois said she used to see them more when she was a kid. She thinks they're endangered."

It wouldn't surprise me. So many species had either gone extinct or become endangered after the Great Eruption.

"How come they ingested whatever is causing the Green Death, but I haven't?" He stacked a pile of plates and placed them in a cardboard box. "I live over in Whitehead, and I know we've had most of the deaths there."

"Yes, Whitehead's been hardest hit."

"Aunt Lois and Leesa used to live there, too. I thought they were safe in Oglethorpe." He gave his head a dismayed shake. "Nobody's ever safe from anything. Safety is an illusion."

"They moved here a couple years ago?"

He nodded. "After Uncle Randolph died, Aunt Lois decided she wanted a change. Leesa wasn't married so they decided to live here together."

"How often did you visit?"

"Once a week or so, depending on my schedule. I work as a handyman, so it's fairly flexible. Aunt Lois liked me to bring her favorite pastry from Lunar Café and a couple bottles of water whenever I visited."

I frowned. "Why water?"

He smiled. "She said Oglethorpe water tasted like armpit sweat. She missed the taste of the Whitehead spring, so she had me bring a couple bottles with me, and she'd save them. Only drank them on special occasions or with visitors."

My veins turned to ice. "And did she have visitors this week?"

"No, it was her birthday, though." He sighed. "At least she got to celebrate before she died."

My whole body felt rigid. "Do you happen to recall the last time you went to the spring for water for Lois?"

He appeared thoughtful. "She told me she had a couple bottles saved from my last visit." He licked his lips, thinking. "Guess that would be about eight or nine days ago."

"Did you notice a strange smell when you were at the spring?"

He scratched his cheek. "A smell? Not that I recall. Then again, that was right after the bar fight with Tom Duncan. Bastard broke my nose. I had to see the healer twice. I couldn't smell or taste anything until the other day."

The Whitehead spring was near the cobbler's stone barn, where Xavier Joyce worked. He lived in Berthold and packed his lunches, but he would've drunk water from the spring. I'd bet good money that every victim drank water from there. Something had contaminated the water source. I had to figure out what.

Landon angled his head. "If you see anything you like the looks of inside, feel free to take it. I need to unload everything except the furniture. There's a family moving in next week."

"Already?"

"Yeah, they've been sharing a house with another family ever since theirs burnt down, so this'll be a nice change for them."

I wandered into the house and spotted a knitted blanket folded on the sofa in pale blues and pinks. "Who had a baby?"

"Aunt Lois knitted that when Leesa was younger,

thinking she might eventually have a baby." Landon's face clouded over. "Leesa didn't really want kids anyway."

"Would you mind if I took it? I know someone who's expecting."

His whole face lit up. "Really? I think Aunt Lois would be thrilled if that blanket ended up with an actual baby instead of an imaginary one."

I tucked the blanket under my arm. "It's going to a good home, I promise."

"Look around. Whatever you take, you'll save me from carting it somewhere else."

I had plenty of experience distributing wealth. "Let me know if you need help. I have special sacks that hold a lot of weight. I can send a few your way."

Landon looked at me. "Thanks. That's kind of you." He gripped the edge of the box. "Say, do you ever spend time in Whitehead? I'd love to meet up sometime."

His question startled me. "Oh, that's nice of you, but I don't think so."

He wore a half smile. "Who's the lucky one?"

"It isn't that. I just have a complicated life. I find it best not to involve anybody in it, if I can help it." And Landon was human. At least werewolves could hold their own against vampires. Someone like Landon would be dead within a week.

His head bobbed. "Well, you're young. I hope it gets less complicated for you."

"Thanks." Although the only way my life would become less complicated was for me to die. What a cheerful thought.

I left the house with the blanket and hurried back to the hideout. It was getting late, but I fully intended to gather the crew and head over to the Whitehead spring to block public access. We couldn't risk anybody else drinking from it until we cleared it of whatever contaminant was lurking there. I'd get a sample and send it to Frank and Mauve for examination, too.

Finally, I had good news to deliver. It was about damn time.

•

Chapter Fifteen

My upbeat mood dissipated when I arrived at the hideout. The crew was gathered at the campfire in a tight huddle speaking in hushed tones. I didn't need to ask to know something was very wrong. Scarlet was the first one to notice me.

"We have a situation," she said.

I removed my quiver and bow and set them against one of the large rocks that served as a seat. "Tell me."

Bear elbowed his way through the group. His eyes shone with unshed tears. "Bonnie's sick."

My whole body tensed. "Sick?"

He wiped a stray tear from his cheek. "It's the Green Death."

I glanced at the knitted blanket tucked under my arm. "How?"

He shook his head. "Hell if I know. She and I went to Whitehead earlier. We shared a meal, so it wasn't the food."

"Where is she now?"

"In bed resting. Drinking lots of water to stay hydrated. I don't know what else to do."

Drinking lots of water. Shit.

"You said you shared a meal in Whitehead. What did you drink?"

"I had a couple beers, but Bonnie didn't want any because of our sprouting bean."

"I think we should relocate the hideout until..." Tyson trailed off.

"It isn't contagious," I told him. "We can stay."

"You're not a scientist. You don't know that for sure." He didn't sound angry, just upset.

"As a matter of fact, I do know." I pivoted to Bear. "I need to talk to her. Is that okay?"

His thick brows drew together. "Yeah, of course. Want me to come?"

"No, thanks. Just me." I climbed the makeshift ladder to their tree house. It was slightly lower than mine, which I only noticed due to the number of steps I had to climb. My feet instinctively wanted to keep climbing. I'd never really noticed from the ground and I couldn't see their home from mine. My tree house was set back from the others to afford me privacy, as well as an amazing view of The Wild. Okay, the view wasn't much more than a black blanket, but sometimes I pictured myself opening my hand and lighting up the whole expanse. It was only my imagination, though. I couldn't risk someone noticing the light and tracing it to our hideout.

Bonnie was tucked into the fetal position on a mattress, her hand cradling the slight bulge of her stomach. I hadn't noticed the bump before. The pregnancy was further along than I realized.

There was a sprinkling of lesions on her face and hands. The rest of her was covered with either clothing or a blanket.

"Hey, Bonnie." I kneeled beside her.

Her eyes opened. "I thought you were Bear." Her voice was low and slightly hoarse.

"He's at the campfire." I set the blanket beside her. "I brought you a present."

"For me?" Her fingers spread across the blanket. "It's so soft."

"It was knitted by an expert named Lois."

"Thank you, Aster. You didn't have to do that."

I touched her forehead. Hot as a poker. "When did you notice your symptoms?"

"An hour or so ago. I felt feverish, but I thought it might be pregnancy related. Then Bear noticed a spot on my cheek."

"Can you retrace your steps in the past twenty-fours? I need to know where you've been."

"Here most of the time. I only went to Whitehead with Bear to see Mauve. She's been checking my progress and giving me ginger sweets to settle my stomach."

"I saw Mauve earlier. You must've seen her afterward."

"She's surprised I'm still vomiting, although it's been less frequent than it was." Her eyes closed, as though the strain of talking had worn her out.

"Did you eat or drink anything there?"

She spoke with her eyes still closed. "I took a pill. A prenatal vitamin. She gave me a bottle to bring home."

My pulse sped up. "You took the pill with water?"

Her eyes popped open. "No, with whiskey. Of course with water."

A flash of the old Bonnie. She was still in there, fighting for dominance.

"Where did Mauve get the water?"

"Her tap was broken, so she took a bottle from the

181

icebox. She said she always refills the bottles from the spring as her emergency supply."

The spring.

I squeezed her hand. "Bonnie, you just confirmed my theory. The Whitehead spring is contaminated. That's where the Green Death is coming from."

"I don't suppose there's any hope for me and the bean at this point." Tears flowed like wet ribbons down her cheek.

I felt sick to my stomach. They didn't have long. Two days at the most. "It's going to be okay, Bonnie."

"Liar," she said, and closed her eyes.

I returned to the campfire, unsure how to comfort Bear. "I'm so sorry."

He glanced at their tree house. "You see them right—the green lesions? I didn't imagine them?"

"No, you didn't. If it's any consolation, I know the source of the disease now. I'm going to head over there now and see if I can close it off."

"Anything I can do to help?" Hugo asked.

"There might be."

Hattie jumped to her feet. "I want to help, too."

Bear stayed behind with Bonnie, while the rest of us stuffed ourselves into the Beast and drove to the far end of Whitehead.

"Ever hear a movie called *Soylent Green*?" Tyson asked.

"Can't say that I have."

"The main character discovers they've been grinding humans into food, and they run around trying to get people to stop eating ... other people."

"Sounds delightful," I commented.

"That's kind of what we're doing."

I arched an eyebrow. "Nobody's eating people. The Green Death isn't *Soylent Green*."

"No, but we're going door-to-door to tell people to stop drinking from the spring or they'll die." He shrugged. "Kind of the same."

"Why doesn't the water smell bad?" Hattie asked.

"I don't know," I said. "Maybe it does now, but it didn't when people first drew the contaminated water from the spring."

"But then someone would've noticed the smell since then," Tyson countered.

"I don't think it's heavily used," I told him. "It's on the outskirts of the village. Most people there seem to get their water from other sources."

"Then why didn't the bottled water stink?" Scarlet pressed. "Bonnie wouldn't drink something that smelled bad."

"I don't have all the answers, okay?" I blurted. "All I know is the spring is the culprit. I don't know why or how or anything else."

"This is my fault," Hattie said. "I wished for this, and it came true."

Scarlet patted her hand. "No, you didn't. Nobody did."

We spilled out of the Beast and swarmed the village square.

"Everybody split up," I said. "Knock on every door. If they use the spring, tell them to find another water source. If they have bottles or jugs in the house that they may have filled from the spring, they need to dump them. Somebody tell Mauve she's got bad bottles and find out if she served them to anybody else today." Poor Mauve would never forgive herself.

"Can they pour them out on the soil?" Tyson asked. "Won't that contaminate the groundwater?"

"Good point. Tell them to dump it back in the spring. That's where I'm going now."

The Whitehead spring didn't stink, which made our job more difficult. Scarlet helped me put up signs all around the spring. Danger. Green Death. Do Not Drink. Any warning we could think of to keep people away. We'd drain the spring if we had to, but this would at least put a stop to the deaths.

Almost.

"I can't stop thinking about Bonnie," Scarlet said.

"I know. If only I'd figured it out sooner."

Tyson arrived at the spring with his hands clenched at his sides. "I almost wish Hattie *had* wished for this." His voice cracked with emotion, which was so unlike him.

I swiveled toward him, aghast. "Why?"

"Because that would mean there's also a way to wish for it to stop."

I froze.

"Aster?" Scarlet said. "Are you okay?"

"Can you finish up here? There's something I need to do."

"Now?"

I broke into a run. "There's someone I need to see," I called over my shoulder.

Someone who could make wishes come true—as long as I didn't die first.

"Are you certain you want to do this?" Ingrid asked.

"Yes."

"Do you know how to fight the creature?"

"I know as much as I possibly can thanks to Hattie." Whether that would be enough remained to be seen.

Ingrid sprinkled a mixture of herbs in a circle on the ground. "Would you be terribly offended if I don't stick around to watch you die?"

"I was going to suggest that anyway." With Ingrid there, she could accidentally become the target. There was another reason I needed Ingrid to go, though. One I couldn't divulge to her.

A cold wind rushed through the clearing, shaking the leaves off the trees, not that they could spare them.

"That's my cue," Ingrid said. "Good luck, Aster."

"Thanks for your help."

"If anyone asks, I had nothing to do with the summoning. I refuse to be responsible for your death."

I clapped my hands in prayer position and bowed. "Consider yourself absolved."

The leaves lifted off the ground and swirled around my ankles. My skin tingled with anticipation. Or maybe it was fear.

With my quiver strapped to my back, I rushed to a nearby thicket and climbed in the middle of it to keep my body hidden. I crossed my legs and worked to slip into a meditative state as quickly as possible. I calmed myself, focusing on separating my physical self from my spirit self. My astral form arrived in the clearing just as Corentine shimmered into existence. Her white curls were as wild as ever. She wore the same white duster and matching boots.

She delivered a cold smile when she saw me. Red flames flickered in her eyes. "We've met before."

"We have."

"And yet you summoned me, knowing what I can do?"

"I need a favor."

She began to circle me. "Fascinating. Most people are terrified of running into me."

"I'm not most people."

"What's the favor?"

"I'll tell you after I win."

She released a shrill cackle. "Such pluck. I do appreciate a worthy adversary."

I felt my heart thrum all the way from the thicket. "Then you'll fight me?"

"I never turn down an opportunity to feed, dear heart. My appetite is limitless." She stopped walking and assessed me. "Something feels wrong."

Before I could respond, she lunged. Her arms thrashed as though I might escape her clutches.

Except I wasn't in them.

The demon paused to stare at her hands and then at me. A question formed on her lips.

I wiggled my fingers. "Surprise."

"That's cheating!"

"No. That's leveling the playing field."

She floated away from me. "You're not a ghost, which means your body must be nearby." She began peering between trees. "Come out, come out wherever you are," she sang.

"I'm right here. Fight me."

She ignored me, continuing the search for my physical form. It was the only way she could win.

"Corentine!"

She ignored me, determined to find my physical form. The demon was getting dangerously close to the thicket. No, no, no. I had to get there before she did.

I focused on my body and let it pull me back inside. By the time I opened my eyes, Corentine had me by the throat. I couldn't breathe. I tried to grip her wrist but my hand smacked empty air. How was she able to make contact with me when I couldn't make contact with her?

Brilliant plan, Aster. A for effort.

Three figures cut through the darkness. Two males and a female. They wore unfamiliar clothing made of metal and leather. If I had to guess, I'd say they were warriors. Corentine noticed them, too.

"Travelers," the demon spat. She released her hold on me and turned to confront them.

The warriors seemed to glide toward us. It took me a second to realize that they, too, were incorporeal. Had I accidentally summoned more demons? The way my day was going, it wouldn't surprise me.

The tallest warrior brandished a sword and sliced right through my opponent. I didn't expect the sword to have any effect given Corentine's state. To my surprise, her body sparked with reddish-orange light. Was that how she bled?

"No," she shrieked. "It isn't fair!" Her translucent figure appeared to solidify. Whatever the warrior had done, Corentine was now corporeal.

I seized the opportunity and notched an arrow, aiming the tip at her head. "On your knees, demon."

Corentine snapped her teeth.

"On your knees, I said."

The trio of warriors crowded around us with their weapons drawn. Their presence alone was menacing. The glinting blades sealed the deal.

Slowly, Corentine dropped to her knees with her hands folded behind her head.

"Who are you?" I asked the warriors.

"We are the Nunnehi," the tallest warrior said to me. "Spirits that travel this land."

I thought of my astral form. "Spirits like me?" I pictured

a group of warriors seated cross-legged in a circle some-where in the forest.

"No, child. We have no physical bodies, nor have we ever." He angled his head toward Corentine. "We are only permitted to intervene in this realm when circumstances warrant it."

Corentine's eyes blazed with fury. "She's mine! I demand justice."

"You know the rules, demon," the warrior said in a cool and collected tone. I got the distinct impression this wasn't their first rendezvous.

Corentine hissed but remained in her submissive pose.

The warrior nodded at me. "Ask your favor, and it shall be granted."

I drew a deep breath and looked at the demon. "I would like you to save Bonnie and her unborn child from the Green Death."

The demon stared at me, unblinking. "The favor isn't for you?"

"No."

"Who is this Bonnie to you? Wife? Lover?"

"She's..." In truth, Bonnie wasn't even a friend, but it didn't matter. She was part of my crew. If there was some-thing I could do to save her, then I owed it to everyone to try. "She's family."

"Do it," the warrior said.

Corentine glowered at the Nunnehi before turning back to me. "Consider it done, but never summon me again. You won't survive a second time."

"Why don't you avoid that possibility by relocating? I hear the Yukon is nice this time of year."

Corentine shimmered, and her form dissipated.

I pivoted to the Nunnehi and bowed. "I don't know how to thank you."

"Continue your good deeds," the female warrior said.

I smiled. "I'm not sure vampires would describe them as good deeds."

"You've demonstrated selflessness. A worthy quality to our kind."

"But you only learned that after I asked for my favor."

The Nunnehi exchanged glances. "We have seen more than you know," the other male warrior said. "We are always here ... in spirit." He smiled at his own joke.

A memory stirred. Poco's reading. I'd bet good money these were the 'shadows' she saw looking out for me.

"If you're always lurking like friendly ghosts, is there any chance you can tell me how this Green Death started so I can make sure it doesn't happen again?"

"Maybe that should have been your favor," the female warrior said, not unkindly.

She was right. I'd been so focused on Bonnie that it hadn't occurred to me to use my favor for the greater good. Some selfless witch I was.

"Is that your way of telling me you don't know?" I asked.

"We're not gods," the tallest one said. "We don't have an all-seeing eye. We've simply traveled The Wild long enough to see you in action."

"We're only permitted to intercede in certain kinds of conflicts," the other male warrior added.

"Like a fight to the death with a demon?" I asked.

He nodded. "Exactly."

"Who makes these rules?" I grumbled.

"Not us," the tallest one said. "We each have a role to

play in the fate of the world. Ours was to make sure you were spared."

His response caught me off guard. "Because I'm the Hooded One?"

The Nunnehi started to back away.

"Our time on this plane has reached an end," the female warrior said.

I opened my mouth to object, but they were already gone. I didn't waste another second. I raced to the hideout to see whether Corentine had fulfilled her promise.

I was spent by the time I reached the hideout. All I wanted to do was stand under the waterfall for an hour and wash away the stench of death and decay. If my aching muscles were soothed in the process, bonus points. But first I needed to know whether my demonic rendezvous had been worth it.

The crew was gathered at the base of Bear and Bonnie's tree house. That could be good or bad.

I snagged Scarlet's gaze, and she shrugged. Hugo paced back and forth like a caged animal.

"Where have you been?" Hattie demanded. "Bonnie's been on death's door and you just up and left." Her cheeks were flushed with anger, and her eyes were rimmed with red from wiping away tears.

Bear poked his head out of the tree house. "Um, everybody?"

I swallowed the lump in my throat and looked at him expectantly.

"Bonnie's lesions are gone, and her fever broke." He broke into a broad smile. "I don't understand it, but she seems to be improving."

"It's a miracle," Hattie breathed.

Scarlet cocked an accusatory eyebrow at me. "Is it?"

I offered a small smile. "I think it qualifies."

"Can we get more water up here? She finished the last pouch."

"On the way." Hattie scrambled to the storage unit for more water.

A few minutes later, Bonnie emerged from the tree house. "I feel fine. I'd like to come down to eat with everyone, if that's okay."

I leaned over to Scarlet and whispered, "She didn't say to eat everyone, right?"

"With," Scarlet emphasized. "Group activity."

I relaxed. Bonnie was alive. She would have her bean. I bit my lip to keep the emotions from spilling out of me.

Hattie met Bonnie at the base of the tree with a pouch of water. Bonnie thanked her in return.

"You look good as new, Bon," Tyson commented.

"I feel pretty good considering I was knocking on death's door an hour ago."

Bear rubbed her stomach. "We should get you to Mauve to check on the bean."

"The bean is fine," she insisted and patted his hand.

"How can you be so sure?" he asked.

"A mother knows." She sauntered toward the campfire. "What's for dinner? I could eat a mountain lion."

"Um, I don't think that's on the menu," Tyson said.

Bear gave us a helpless shrug. "She's eating for two, remember?"

Chapter Sixteen

I awoke the next day feeling better than I had in ages. The Whitehead spring was blocked off. Bonnie and her bean were alive and thriving. Life wasn't so bad in The Wild.

It was still early when I climbed down the ladder. I figured I'd sneak in a shower at the waterfall before anyone could beat me to it. Hugo was on watch, but I didn't see him as I crept away from the hideout.

On the path toward the waterfall, a foul odor reached my nostrils. I sniffed the air. It was possible the stench of the Green Death had clung to my clothing. I lifted my sleeve to my nose and inhaled.

Nope.

I breathed in the putrid smell again and attempted to follow my nose. If my waterfall was contaminated, too, there would be hell to pay. I deserved a relaxing shower.

I pictured a sick villager stumbling through the forest in a desperate attempt to stop the disease from spreading. Just because I'd explained it was a contaminated water supply didn't mean they all believed it. Human beings could be stubborn.

I stepped over fallen trees until I reached a hollow log. The smell was stronger here. I bent over to inspect the log. It was too dark to see inside, so I opened my hand and allowed a bit of light to illuminate the interior. My breathing hitched when I spotted several glass bottles lined along the bottom of the log. This was no random placement. Someone had hidden these bottles here.

I picked up a couple leaves and used them in place of gloves. I didn't dare risk touching the bottles without protection. I reached for the closest one and withdrew it for a closer inspection. Although it was empty, I didn't need to remove the lid to know which substance had once been contained within it. I could still smell the foul odor. My blood began to boil when I realized that I recognized the design. I'd seen this bottle before, and I knew exactly where. I slipped the bottle in my pocket and abandoned my quest for a shower. Poco said someone would betray me, and I'd wondered who.

Now I knew.

Questions pelted my brain as I marched back to the hideout, but there was only person who could answer them, and that person wasn't me.

I stopped when I reached the edge of the clearing. Hugo was alone. His brow lifted in surprise.

"I didn't see you leave."

"Then I guess you weren't doing your job very well. Care to explain this?" I held out the empty bottle for examination.

His gaze darted to the empty bottle and back to me. "I don't know what you mean."

"This is your potion bottle. I recognize it. It's the reason why you wanted a new one from the loot we collected from the tax collector."

He gave an awkward laugh. "Is it?"

I leveled him with a look. "You know it is. You also know that it smells like the Green Death because you're the one who created the poisonous potion."

"Don't be absurd. Why on earth would I poison all those people? I'm not the one who treats them like vermin."

"A vampire has no reason to kill people this way. It makes no sense, and you know it."

His body shook with anger. "They're monsters. It doesn't have to make sense."

"How did you make the potion? Did you use the ginger and windflower that you stole from the Lunar Cafe?"

He flinched. "I don't know anything about missing plants."

I stared at him in disbelief. It was Hugo. I was certain of it. "You're the one who torched the donation center, aren't you? Did you wear my cloak to do it?" He'd wanted them to think it was me. "Why would you do that?"

His face hardened. "You were getting too close. I didn't expect you to dig in and become The Wild's version of Sherlock Holmes."

"So you deliberately tried to get me out of the way by putting vampire heat on me."

"My plan needed more time to come to fruition."

"Why? What's your endgame?" I thought of his poorly planned attack in Remy's Bog. Maybe he was simply a sociopath.

"I thought the Green Death would convince people that it's time to rise up against Lord Doran and the crown, against all vampires. We need to make a stand."

The realization settled over me. This was the reason,

plainly stated. "You're trying to force another uprising instead of waiting for the right time."

He waved his hands in anger and frustration. "What is this mythical right time of which you speak? They will continue to drain people of their blood. They will continue to oppress us and steal from us until we fight back."

"You know the history of The Wild. You know what happens when a rebellion is staged without sufficient planning. I lost my own grandmother that way. Our coven was destroyed. Don't be a fool."

Hugo sneered at me. "I think you've misjudged which one of us is the fool." He pulled an object from his pocket and tossed it at me.

I tried to dodge it, but I wasn't fast enough. I crashed to the ground, and a sharp pain shot up my arm. Then everything went black.

Hugo had betrayed me. He'd betrayed us all.

When I opened my eyes, I was on a bed. My wrists sported inhibitor cuffs, which were basically bracelets that cut off my access to my magic, but I was otherwise unshackled. The interior of the room was nicer than anywhere I'd ever slept in my life. There were no windows, but that wasn't unusual for a building constructed during the Eternal Night.

I ran to the door and found it locked. I pounded on the heavy wood until it opened. I hauled off and swung a fist at my captor.

Lord Doran caught my hand and pushed it gently back to my side. His frame filled the doorway, effectively blocking my path.

"You're awake," he said.

"Where am I?"

"The White Fortress."

The secret stronghold had a name.

"Why am I in a fairly nice room and not a dungeon?"

The hint of a smile showed on his face. "You'd prefer the dungeon, would you? I mean, to each their own, of course."

"Why am I here?"

He gave me a pointed look. "Come now, Miss Goodfellow. You know why."

"Whatever Hugo told you is a lie to save his own skin. What's the deal you struck with him?"

"We pardoned his former crimes with the agreement that he would bring us the Hooded One. It seems that would be you."

"That wizard you negotiated with is the cause of the Green Death. He's responsible for multiple deaths, including the death of your three vampires." I stared at him. "Did you really lose three vampires to the Green Death or was that a lie?"

"It seems we've both been dishonest with each other."

"I'm not lying. Hugo set me up. He kept trying to sideline me so I wouldn't discover the truth about the Green Death."

Doran looked down at me. "You solved the mystery of the Green Death."

"I did."

"Why not deliver the news to me as we discussed? I might've rewarded your hard work."

"I didn't do it for a reward."

His eyes seemed to pierce my very essence. "I would've liked to hear from you directly ... so that I could ask questions."

"Well, I'm here now." I wiggled my fingers through the cuffs. "You have my full attention."

The light faded from his eyes. "Yes, you're here now. Unfortunately, the circumstances are quite different." He cleared his throat. "Are you or are you not the Hooded One?"

"I didn't burn down your donation center, if that's what you're really asking. Hugo did that, too."

He exhaled in frustration. "There's an easier way to settle this." He poked his head through the doorway and spoke to someone out of view before turning back to me.

A woman entered the room behind him. Average height. Slender build. No weapons. Her dark brown hair was tied in a braid. Her black and red cloak seemed slightly too big, as though she'd inherited it from an older sibling.

"This is my aura reader, Christina. I keep her on staff to determine whether anyone is lying to me."

My throat grew dry. "Sounds like someone has trust issues."

Christina focused her brown eyes on me. "Have a seat, Miss Goodfellow. You might as well make yourself comfortable."

"That's hard when you've got metal bracelets that are too small for comfort." Still, I sat on the edge of the bed.

"Are you the Hooded One?" Christina stayed in place, but I could feel her tendrils of magic attempting to penetrate my mind.

"No," I said firmly.

"Are you responsible for any ambushes or robberies in The Wild?"

"No."

"Did you burn down the donation center in Klondike?"

"No."

She probed and prodded for another few minutes until Doran grew impatient.

"Well?" he prompted.

"She's being truthful," Christina said.

Doran blinked in surprise. Clearly, he'd been expecting a different answer. "Thank you, Christina."

I resisted the urge to breathe a sigh of relief. I had no idea why Christina would lie on my behalf. The witch connection wasn't enough. Plenty of witches and wizards were only too happy to garner favors and steady employment from our vampire overlords. No doubt Christina had a cushy job with his lordship.

Hope surged through me. "Then I'm free to go?"

"Not quite. Apparently, Lord Birney has his own version of Christina. I'll see if they've arrived." He left the room.

Christina frowned at me. "How did you do it?"

"Do what?"

"Cloak your aura."

"I didn't. I wouldn't know how to do that."

"I've never been unable to read someone."

I shrugged. "What can I say? There's a first time for everything."

Christina continued to scrutinize me. "What kind of magic do you possess?"

"The diluted kind. Rumor has it my real father was human."

Once again, she seemed to buy the lie. "I know what you're thinking. How can I betray my kind by working for him? The truth is he isn't the monster people believe."

I didn't bother to hold back a snort.

"No, really. He's done so much good for The Wild. People have no idea. It's Lord Birney you need to avoid.

He's the real monster." She shuddered. "Lord Doran issued an order that no member of staff is permitted to be left alone with him, that's how bad he is."

"Lord Doran also issues orders that execute innocent people in retaliation for something they didn't do. If that doesn't count as monstrous, then I don't know what does."

Her expression crumpled. "That was Lord Birney's order. One of his worst yet."

"Why didn't Doran stop him?"

She lowered her gaze. "I'm not saying he's perfect. I'm only telling you that he's more complex than he appears."

"Sounds like somebody has a bit of a crush. Maybe you want to let him know. I hear he's single."

"Single but not available. He took his family's death quite hard. I don't think he's ever fully recovered."

"What happened to them?"

Before she could answer, Doran returned to the room. "You may go, Christina."

"And me?" I asked.

"Your presence is required elsewhere." He edged closer to me. His presence seemed to fill the room. "I wasn't completely honest with you before."

My throat tightened. "About what?"

"I said I was disappointed that you didn't contact me with an update on the Green Death."

"Yes." I held his gaze.

"I was disappointed because I realized I wanted to see you again," he said.

He towered over me now. Any closer and our bodies would be touching. A voice inside me urged me forward. I resisted. The longer I looked at him, the more handsome he became. My esophagus burned with revulsion. How could I possibly think such a thing? Doran was a vampire and not just any vampire. He was responsible for my grandmother's death and the destruction of my coven. Maybe he could be kind like Christina insisted, but he could also be cruel. If you had to roll the dice to see which Doran you'd get, it wasn't a game worth playing. There were enough good men out there that didn't come with such brutal baggage.

I lifted my chin. "And you decided the best way to achieve that was to take me prisoner?"

"An accusation was made. Evidence was provided. I had no choice. But look on the bright side, I could've shackled you to a wall in a cell, but I didn't."

It seemed like a good time to remind him of his own treachery. "You set me up the last time we spoke. You made sure Audra mentioned the delivery to Fairbanks in front of me. You weren't interested in collaborating on the Green Death. You only wanted to bait me."

His mouth twitched. "I admit that was the original plan." Strong hands slid down my forearms, setting off alarm bells as well as a pleasant shiver. "And, for what it's worth, I'm sorry I misjudged you."

"What will you do to me?"

"I'm honestly still deciding." He lowered his lips to mine.

"Excuse me, my lord," a chirpy voice interrupted.

He released my body so abruptly that I nearly toppled over. Only the vampire's quick reflexes prevented me from falling.

"What is it, Marcy? I believe I asked not to be disturbed."

The petite vampire lowered her gaze to the floor. "I'm so sorry, sir. Lord Birney says your special guest has arrived."

Doran's face hardened. I couldn't decide whether he

was angry with Marcy for interrupting us or angry with himself for being tempted by me. Possibly both.

"Marcy, please escort Miss Goodfellow to the club room."

"Right this way, miss," Marcy said.

"Take her via the south wing," Doran instructed.

Marcy nodded. Her features were almost childlike in their daintiness. Each of her long fingernails was painted a different color. She escorted me to a room at the end of a long, stone corridor.

"I'm seriously confused right now," I said. "Why was I not in a dungeon?"

"I don't know, but I can tell you Lord Doran specifically requested that bedroom for you. His chambers are right next door."

I started to cough. "Why? Why would he put me so close to his private chambers?" Part of me wondered whether this was another attempt to get me to lower my guard and show my hand. Maybe his earlier behavior had been another ruse.

Marcy lowered her voice. "I suspect it's on account of Lord Birney. Lord Doran doesn't trust him. To be fair, I don't blame him. I'd hate to think what Lord Birney did for the king to earn his appointment. You don't become Earl of the Outer Territories by fostering kittens."

No, you certainly didn't.

"Not all the rooms are available for use yet," Marcy continued. "The fortress is still unfinished. It was supposed to be done by now, but Lord Doran had to reallocate materials elsewhere."

I remembered his complaints about the king's budget and wondered whether that had played a role.

Marcy turned around to face me when she reached the

closed door. "I know this all seems very relaxed, but you should know that there are guards patrolling this fortress all day every day. Some of them are invisible." She offered a shy smile. "Just thought you'd be interested in that."

"Thank you." I appreciated her candor. Even if I managed to break down a door or overpower Marcy, I faced a dozen obstacles between here and freedom. If I couldn't use my magic, I was at a severe disadvantage. I'd have to wait and see how this played out. Doran was hard to read and impossible to trust. One minute he seemed to want to kiss me and the next minute he was Lord Doran, Thegn of The Wild.

Opening the door, she dipped her head and left.

"Miss Goodfellow, come in," a voice called.

I crossed the threshold to see Lord Birney seated in a plush chair across from another vampire. Each held a glass of blood while a fire roared in the hearth.

"Isn't this cozy?" I said.

"I'd like you to meet our esteemed guest," the earl said. "Miss Aster Goodfellow, meet Vincent Dufresne, Master Inquisitor."

Chapter Seventeen

The door slammed shut behind me.

The name meant nothing to me. "Friend of yours?"

Lord Birney frowned. "I said he's the Master Inquisitor."

I studied the visiting vampire. He wore a charcoal-colored suit and a black shirt with a red tie. His fangs looked surprisingly small and delicate for a vampire his size. "I don't know what that is."

A small smile appeared. "Don't worry, you will," Birney said.

His response unnerved me.

The door opened, and Doran entered the room behind me. "Master Inquisitor, this is an honor. Thank you for traveling all this way."

The visitor rose to his feet to shake Doran's hand. "Please, you may call me Vincent. I've always desired to see this part of the world. Lord Birney's invitation was the perfect excuse to make the journey."

Doran gestured to me. "And I assume you've met the reason for your visit."

My throat constricted. *I* was the reason for this vampire's visit? I tried to disguise my shock, not wanting to give them the satisfaction.

Vincent assessed me. "I've been apprised of the situation. I'm intrigued, I must admit." He cut a glance at Birney. "Do you intend to drink from her as well or is this purely informational?"

I'd like to see him try.

"Information is all we need," Doran said. "Though my aura reader has already determined..."

Birney held up a hand. "The Master Inquisitor can tell us far more than whether she's the Hooded One. It can offer us a glimpse of her true power."

A shiver rattled my body. They were going to dissect me like a lab rat.

"What makes you think I have any?" I asked.

They ignored me.

"It must've taken you quite some time to get here," Doran said.

"I only traveled by land part of the way. I used the services of a portal witch in Minneapolis."

"You were able to portal to the White Fortress?" Dorian inquired. "That's an impressive feat."

"Oh no. She managed to get me as far as Anchorage, and I traveled the rest of the way by..." He paused. "What do you call your specialized vehicles again?"

"Beasts," Doran offered.

Vincent smiled. "Yes, we traveled the rest of the way by Beast. My lower back is not a fan." He made a show of rubbing the injured spot.

"A bit more blood will help with that." Birney raised a glass. "Doran, would you like a drink before we get started?"

"No, thank you."

Birney drank the remainder of the blood and set down the glass. "What do you need from us, Mr. Dufresne?"

Vincent requested the key to my inhibitor cuffs.

"Is that wise?" Birney asked.

"It'll ruin the sample if her magic is being suppressed. I need it flowing freely through her veins."

"But we have no idea what she's capable of. If she truly is the Hooded One, I've heard rumors..." The earl looked at me with a mixture of concern and derision.

"She isn't the Hooded One," Doran interrupted. "My aura reader confirmed it."

"That's why I'm here," Vincent said smoothly. "To confirm or deny. She'll be shackled to the wall, so unless her magic involves brute strength, she isn't going anywhere."

"Wouldn't stop her from hurting you, though," Birney said.

Vincent remained impassive. "I'll take my chances."

Birney nodded and produced the key. "I'll leave you to it then. Let me know when you have an answer. I'd like to make a public spectacle of her, the sooner, the better."

"Certainly."

Birney crossed the room. "Let's go, Doran. Our presence isn't required here."

Doran shifted uneasily.

Birney gave me a hard shove toward Vincent. "Don't stand there like an imbecile. Let him shackle you."

I ground my teeth. Vincent guided me across the room like he'd just punched my dance card. We arrived at the far wall where a set of chains awaited me. He secured my legs first, then removed my inhibitor cuffs before adding my arms to the chains. "I'd prefer a rack for this, but we play the hand we're dealt, don't we?"

I debated whether to use my magic.

Vincent seemed to read my thoughts. "I wouldn't advise any sudden moves. Even if you kill me and manage to extract yourself from the shackles, which I doubt you can, there are a dozen vampires right outside the door. And there are a dozen more between here and the nearest exit. The fortress itself is in the middle of nowhere. You wouldn't get very far."

He removed his suit jacket with finesse and hung it on the back of a chair, dusting off the shoulders.

"What exactly do you intend to do to me?"

He stooped to root through what looked like a well-worn medical bag. "No need for questions. All will be revealed momentarily." He produced a small knife. "This won't hurt too much. Just a tiny prick." He held the blade between us. "Or would you prefer I use my fangs? Your choice."

"Why do you need my blood?"

"Normally, I begin with a series of questions, but Lord Birney is rather impatient, so he's asked me to cut to the quick, no pun intended." He smiled. "Your blood should reveal everything I need to know."

"You have that kind of technology?" I asked.

"I'm the Master Inquisitor," he said, as though that answered my question.

"Keep your fangs off me."

"Very well. Blade it is." He set a copper bowl on the floor in front of my right arm and sliced open my forearm. Blood seeped from the wound.

I suppressed a whimper as the crimson liquid spilled into the bowl.

"Your blood has a delicious smell. Has anybody ever told you that?" He leaned over the copper bowl and inhaled. "I think I might take a little extra for myself."

He let the wound drain before moving the bowl to my left arm and making another cut.

"You should've brought extra bowls," I told him, trying to maintain a casual tone.

"I have my own little ritual."

I swallowed the lump in my throat. I wish I knew what effect my magic would have on the metal shackles, if any. I wouldn't mind killing Vincent, but I didn't want to kill dozens of vampires between here and freedom who might not want to kill me. Not to mention, if word got out about my magic, I'd be hunted by every vampire in the world. They'd consider me a threat to their entire species. The longer I concealed it, the better my chance of survival. Maybe there was another way.

If I couldn't physically escape, I could at least send my astral form to identify an escape route should I manage to flee. It would keep me distracted from this torture and give me hope. A win-win.

I concentrated on separating my astral form from my physical one. Vincent wouldn't know what was happening to me. He'd simply think I was trying to block the experience from my mind.

I peeled away from my body and remained crouched behind it until Vincent turned away. My astral form dropped through the floor into the room below. I glided along corridors, noting the layout of the fortress. I traveled through large, arched doorways and along stone staircases. If I spied any vampires, I disappeared through a wall until they were gone.

The furnishings were almost nonexistent, but this place

wasn't built for comfort. I found my way to the parapet and floated to the front of the White Fortress. The stronghold was nothing like I expected. Despite the impressive name, I still envisioned a small outpost at the base of the mountain. The structure in front of me, however, was far from small. Built into the side of the White Mountains, it was essentially a fortified gorge complete with walls, towers, and a gatehouse. Only part of the fortress was visible. The remainder was hidden away inside the mountain. How long had it taken the vampires to create this, and how had its construction escaped our notice? So much for our scouting abilities.

I turned to identify the surroundings when I spotted a moving mass where no mass should be. I floated as far as the cord between my forms extended. Too far and I'd involuntarily snap back to my body.

I squinted at the horizon. They carried flaming torches. Metal glinted. Weapons, too. It was an angry mob, and they were coming to exact revenge on my vampire captors. Hugo's plan was coming to fruition.

I returned to my body to find Vincent slicing open a vein on my neck. Tears dripped from my lashes to my cheeks.

The door burst open, and Lord Doran's frame filled the doorway. "Mr. Dufresne, Lord Birney has asked to see you. He says it's urgent."

Vincent twisted to look at the vampire. "I'm in the middle of a delicate procedure."

Doran didn't seem the least bit interested in the torture I was enduring. "I'm simply following orders, Mr. Dufresne."

"Very well," he muttered. He leaned the knife against

the side of the bowl, then patted my cheek. "Don't go anywhere. I'll be right back."

Doran nodded as the inquisitor passed by. The moment he disappeared into the corridor, Doran rushed forward and unlocked my shackles. He caught me as I pitched forward.

"We need to go."

"Go?" I had trouble focusing on him. I was now acutely aware of the cuts on my body. "Go where?"

"Somewhere safe."

Safe for him or for me?

"Why?" I croaked. It was the only word I could push through my lips.

He helped me to my feet. "Birney arranged for his visit. If I'd known what he intended to do, I would've sent him away sooner, I swear it."

I found my strength returning, along with my dignity. "He's called the Master Inquisitor. How did you think he extracted information? Through charm and wit?"

"He wrote a book about his methods. It seemed like interrogation techniques."

"What difference does it make to you? Why not let him torture the truth out of me?"

He looked away, unable to meet my gaze. "I didn't ... I didn't expect to care."

Hollow laughter escaped me. "Is this another attempt to trick me?"

"I understand why you would wonder, but I promise you that this outcome is as much a surprise to me as it is to you."

"And are you also going to claim you didn't retaliate for the destruction of the donation center by murdering innocent villagers?"

To my surprise, he flinched. "For the record, I didn't order those executions. That was also Lord Birney's handiwork. If I'd known he'd issued the order, I would've overridden it."

And here I'd assumed Doran was the hothead. "You're the thegn."

He glowered at me. "And he's the earl. If I push too hard, you'll have Birney in charge instead of me. Trust me, you don't want that." He grabbed my hand and tugged me toward the corridor.

"You need to get out of here, too," I said, remembering what I'd witnessed outside. Now that he'd released me, I felt obligated to warn him. "There's a mob headed here. If they find you, they'll kill you."

His brow furrowed. "How do you know?"

"It doesn't matter. Just know they're coming.

"They can't touch us here."

"The fortress is warded?"

"Not yet, but it's still a fortress. You're talking about a bunch of unruly people with primitive weapons."

I stared at him. His arrogance didn't surprise me. After all, he'd lived this long without repercussions.

"Hugo used us both. He turned me in to clear the way so he can incite a rebellion against you. He created the Green Death to upset people. He knew that if enough innocent people died, they might finally be willing to rise up against you."

I was beginning to see that Hugo was another kind of monster. One that had even more moral ambiguity than Doran.

"It isn't safe here, no matter what you think," I continued. "Hugo is a wizard. He'll use whatever magic he has at his disposal."

Marcy raced into the room. "My lord, rangers have reported a mob headed this way."

I shot Doran a pointed look.

The vampire didn't flinch. "How could a mob manage to travel all the way to here?"

Marcy wrung her hands. "That I can't say, my lord. What I can tell you is that they're hundreds strong and there are turned wolves among them."

"Wolves are no match for these walls," Doran said.

"Maybe not in and of themselves," she replied, "but there's also signs of magic."

That got his attention. "Is it the Hooded One? Do you see the golden cloak?"

His question took me by surprise. He truly believed I was innocent.

Marcy's head bobbed. "They're leading the charge."

My hands clenched into fists. What was Hugo doing? I started forward. "Show me."

Doran's hand shot out to grasp my sleeve. "Absolutely not. I'm not letting you get caught up in this."

I shook off his grip. "Why not? I'm the enemy, remember? The one you need to dissect."

His fingers tightened on my hand. "A mistake. All a mistake."

The intensity of his tone shook me to my core. Looking into his eyes, I felt an overwhelming sense of calm. Given the current situation, it struck me as an odd sensation.

He snapped at Marcy. "Take her to the bunker. Don't let her out until we're rid of this nuisance and don't tell Birney or Dufresne where she is."

"Yes, my lord."

"Wait!" I ran back for the copper bowl and knife. This was my chance to stop the inquisitor from taking my blood to a lab. I ran to the hearth and tossed the items into the roaring fire.

"Why did you do that?" Doran asked.

"It's the principle," I lied.

We filed into the corridor. Doran hurried one way and Marcy turned in the opposite direction.

I stopped her once the coast was clear. "Marcy, I don't want to hurt you, but I need you to let me go."

Her fangs pressed into her lower lip. "I don't want to hurt you either."

"Good, I'm glad we're in agreement. There are people coming to hurt you. I want you to hide in that bunker."

"What about you?"

"I'm going to see if I can stop them." I didn't want this. I didn't want any of it.

Footsteps thundered, and dozens of guards rushed past us, taking no notice of us. Voices shouted. The attack was underway. Marcy heeded my advice and fled to the bunker.

Remembering my route in astral form, I ran to the parapet. Marcy wasn't exaggerating. I counted hundreds of attackers. At the very front stood Hugo in my golden cloak, along with the rest of my crew. I swore out loud. No doubt Hugo had convinced them to avenge me.

I squinted as a white wolf pushed his way through the mob to the front line. Even from this distance I could tell how large he was. The sight of the majestic creature took my breath away.

Guards and rangers spilled out of the fortress. Explosions rocked the vampires, and they disappeared in a haze of orange smoke.

Hugo had come prepared.

I had to reach my crew. I turned and sprinted to the stone staircase I'd seen in astral form. If I recalled correctly, this one would take me to a side exit. From there, I could run straight to the battlefield.

My breathing was ragged by the time I reached the final corridor. The door at the far end beckoned me. I bolted for the exit.

Fingers grasped the hem of my shirt and yanked me backward. I lost my balance and fell to the floor. I looked straight into the face of Lord Birney.

"Going somewhere, pet?"

I tipped sideways and rolled to my feet. The vampire was faster than he looked. I blinked, and he was in front of me, blocking my path. His fangs elongated and he sprang forward.

"I gave enough blood today, thanks," I ground out, struggling to hold him back. I tried to push his face away without letting my fingers stray too close to his fangs.

"You can't overpower me, witch." He demonstrated his statement by whacking me in the side of the head with such force that my head seemed to ring like a bell. I tasted blood in my mouth. Before I could recover, he grabbed me by the hair and jerked my head to the right, preparing to sink his fangs into my carotid artery.

I struggled to break free, but he was too strong. I used the only defensive move I had left. I raised my hand to his face and unleashed my magic. My skin burned with a brilliant light.

"My eyes!" He released me and covered his face with his arms to block the light. I kept my hand at his eye level, careful not to increase the intensity. The moment he dropped to his knees, I seized the opportunity and ran.

I passed the Master Inquisitor, who simply stood in the shadows of an alcove and regarded me with the flick of an imaginary hat. I wasn't sure why he didn't try to stop me, nor did I care. I was out of the fortress now, and that's all that mattered.

I raced to the battlefield. People were hitting the vampires with everything they had, but it wouldn't be enough. The only real accomplishment would be a slight dent in the vampire population. Doran was right. They'd never get inside the fortress to take control.

Amidst the chaos, I spotted Bonnie in human form. Our eyes met, and we ran to meet halfway. Blood was smeared across her face and chest. I couldn't tell whether it belonged to her or someone else.

"Bonnie, should you be out here fighting?"

"If I'm not going to fight for my bean, then who will?" She noticed a vampire a few yards away and started toward him.

I gripped her arms to hold her in place. "Listen, there's something you need to know. Hugo is responsible for the Green Death. He gave me up to get me out of the way."

It took her a moment to process the information. "Hugo killed those people?"

"Yes. For this." My hand swept the field. "He wanted to force a confrontation. Get people upset enough to fight."

Bonnie's face looked like it had been carved from stone. Her hands moved to cradle her bump. "He nearly killed us."

"And me. He was willing to sacrifice us to get what he wanted. And now he has it."

Her nostrils flared as she turned to scan the battlefield. I'd never seen her shift so quickly. By the time her paws hit the ground, she was full furry.

"Bonnie, wait!"

Howling with rage, she burst through the crowd in search of her prey. I wasn't usually afraid of Bonnie, but I was right now.

Between the darkness and the smoke, it was hard to see. I dodged vampires and jumped over bodies in an effort to find my crew. Unfamiliar wolves paused to look at me and carried on toward their prey.

A rumbling sound drew my attention beyond us. More Beasts rolled onto the field filled with rangers. Someone had summoned reinforcements.

Wolves shot off in all directions when they realized they were outnumbered. I felt adrift. I couldn't see any of my crew in the haze. What if they were injured—or worse?

Bodies littered the earth. Vampires, wolves, humans. Everyone suffered a loss today. I thought of Hecate's Revolt in a new light. I'd assumed my grandmother had been clever and brave—but what if she'd been as foolish and headstrong as Hugo?

I didn't like to think of her that way.

There was no sign of Bear or any other members of the crew. I hoped that was a good sign, that they'd already cut and run.

Surviving vampires fed on the dead. Two of them fled as I approached, and I saw Hugo's mangled body riddled with puncture wounds. The spoils of war.

A few feet away, I spotted my golden cloak on the ground. It had been trampled several times over, but I didn't care. I swiped it off the ground and slipped into it. It felt like home.

The orange smoke was clearing. There were more bodies on the ground than standing. Most of the survivors had fled when the Beasts arrived.

I looked up to see half a dozen rangers headed in my direction. I pivoted right, then left, trying to decide the best route of escape.

The white wolf landed in front of me like a getaway car.

I didn't hesitate. I jumped on his back, wrapping my legs around his torso and gripping his neck with all my strength. The wolf plowed straight through the row of rangers and away from the fortress. I spared a glance over my shoulder and saw Doran on the parapet, observing the carnage. He'd saved me from torture, but that didn't mean he wanted me to escape.

I raised a hand in greeting. He answered me by turning to enter the fortress, his arms rigid at his sides.

He'd seen me in the cloak, I was sure of it. He knew I'd lied. And if he hadn't discovered what I did to Lord Birney, he would soon enough. Whatever trust I'd earned inside the fortress was surely lost now.

The wolf leaped over rocks and down hillsides. Over streams. I could feel his powerful muscles moving in tandem. He ran with such speed that I had to clench my legs against his sides to keep from falling off.

He slowed his pace when we reached a line of trees. From here I could see for miles. There was no one within range. I loosened my grip and slid my feet to the ground.

Bones cracked, joints popped, and fur receded until I found myself face-to-face with Max. Well, inasmuch as you could be face-to-face with a stone tower. "Told you you'd be happy about me following you next time," he said.

"Were we at the same battle? Did you miss the part where I rescued myself?"

"I did. I was too busy saving you to notice."

"You gave me a lift. That's not the same."

"Okay, fine. I saw your mad escape from the fortress. Doesn't it feel good to show off?"

I bristled. "I wasn't showing off."

"Sure you were. You're one of those birds with the

pretty feathers, spreading them wide and preening in front of suitors."

"I think you'll find it's the male birds that have the pretty feathers. The females are usually pretty bland."

He placed a hand on my shoulder. "Don't be so hard on yourself. I don't find you the least bit bland."

I shrugged off his touch. "You should find your pack and get them out of the area." I had no doubt there'd been an emergency call for reinforcements. Rangers would be crawling the region.

"My pack knows where to go. I'm taking you back to your hideout first. That's what you call it, isn't it?"

I stared at him with a stony expression. "How do you know that?"

"I do my homework when the subject interests me."

"You put my whole crew in danger if you tell anybody..."

He held up a hand. "I haven't told anyone, and that includes my pack."

"Well, that's good because your pack seems to include a hundred wolves."

"Closer to two hundred, but who's counting?"

"Were they all here?" It didn't seem like that many wolves.

"No, this was just intel for us. We heard about the mob and tagged along to get the lay of the land." He grinned at me. "Totally worth it."

It was only when I tore my gaze away from his face that I realized he was naked. I slammed my eyes shut and turned around.

"I'm good here. I can find my way home."

"Don't be ridiculous. It'll take you the better part of a day on foot."

I turned back to face him. "We're that far?"

"We are. Come on. You can ride me." His lips curved ever so slightly.

"I appreciate the offer, but I think it's best if we go our separate ways."

"Is this because I'm naked?"

"No, it's because you're obnoxious."

He chuckled. "Now that you're not imprisoned, how about I take you on a date this week? Anywhere you like. The food at the Dancing Dragon is superb, by the way. You have excellent taste."

I burst into laughter. "You can't be serious."

"And you're too serious. That's your problem."

"I don't have a problem."

"Everything is life-and-death with you."

I motioned to the open wound on my neck. "I think you'll find it's warranted."

"You need to decompress. Learn to relax." His mouth twitched. "I'm pretty confident I can help you with that."

I shook my head. "I'm a witch, Max. Find yourself a nice werewolf. The gods know there are plenty of them in The Wild." And plenty who'd be more than happy to mate with someone like Max.

"You're going to need me, Aster." He grinned. "And eventually you're going to want me, too."

Fat chance, blondie.

He spread his arms wide. "Last chance to climb aboard the Max Kane train. Next stop: not-so-secret hideout."

I looked around us. I hated to admit that he was right. It would take me too long on foot, and I ran the risk of getting picked up by rangers.

"Fine," I relented. "But this is as far as this relationship goes."

"Wow. We've progressed to a relationship already? I'm not sure I'm ready for that level of commitment." His body exploded with white fur and powerful muscles. His snout featured a set of sharp teeth designed for tearing flesh and crunching bone. Four massive paws dropped to the ground. His head turned to look at me, those unusual eyes glittering like blue diamonds in the snow.

I didn't like the way his transition made me feel. I'd lived with wolves for years and yet never experienced a physical response to one.

Dammit.

Reluctantly, I climbed on his back and headed for home.

Chapter Eighteen

I sat at the campfire huddled in a blanket. Scarlet and I were the first ones awake. Everybody else was still sleeping off yesterday's battle.

Scarlet handed me a cup of peppermint tea and sat on the rock adjacent to mine. "Your wounds are already healing."

I nodded. "As long as I rest, I'll be like new in a couple days." I paused to blow the steam off my tea. "You told Bonnie that I summoned Corentine, didn't you?"

"What makes you ask that?"

"She tucked me into bed when I got back and offered to spoon-feed me."

Scarlet shrugged. "I thought she might treat you with a little more respect if she knew what you'd been willing to do for her. You're our fearless leader. The crew needs to understand what you risk for us each and every day."

"We all take risks."

"Yours is different, and you know it. You're the pretty face of this little organization." She gave my thigh a gentle smack. "Speaking of telling Bonnie things, why did you tell her about Hugo?"

"Because she deserved to know the truth. We all did."

"Yeah, but you knew what she would do."

I sipped my tea. "I wasn't thinking clearly in the moment. Anyway, what was the alternative?"

She sighed. "You're right. Secrets are bad for the group. If we keep secrets, we destroy trust."

One by one the rest of the crew appeared, drawn to the campfire like moths to a flame. Each one seemed to be more bruised and battered than the last. By now, everybody knew the truth about Hugo.

Tyson smashed his fist into the palm of his hand. "I wish he was still alive so I could kill him all over again."

"He's not only responsible for the Green Deaths," Bear said. "He's responsible for the ones Doran executed over the blood bank."

I swallowed another mouthful of tea, which had already grown lukewarm. "For what it's worth, Birney ordered those executions."

"He was probably passing the buck," Tyson said. "Wanted to gain your trust."

"He isn't the one who told me." I watched the crackling flames, remembering the look on Doran's face when I'd confronted him. "And I believe them." Not that it mattered. Doran was still a vampire responsible for despicable things. He'd let me go, yes, but he'd also put me in that dangerous position in the first place.

"You should've killed Birney when you had the chance," Bonnie said.

"I wasn't thinking clearly. I just wanted to get out of there." I looked at her. "To find all of you."

Bonnie didn't hide her dissatisfaction. "Yeah, well, next time you see him, don't let him go." She looked at me. "That goes for Doran, too. I don't care if he held your hair back when you were barfing up blood, he's a monster. He deserves to die."

I shifted uncomfortably. I didn't want to admit that I was questioning much of what I thought I knew about Doran. About my grandmother. I needed time to think and process what I'd learned.

"I still can't believe the Ghost Pack is real," Bear said, sounding almost dreamy. "Did you see their alpha? He was the size of an oak tree."

I smirked. "Hard to miss him."

"Where do you think they went?" Scarlet asked. "They didn't stick around."

"Yeah, I thought for sure they'd storm the fortress," Bear said. "They were one tough bunch. I saw one wolf wearing an eye patch. I don't know how it doesn't snap in half when he shifts."

Bonnie frowned at him. "Your brain goes to the weirdest places."

He engulfed her in his arms. "That's why you love me."

I excused myself to use the outhouse. On my way back to the campfire, I found Hattie slumped against the base of a tree shining a flashlight on a book in her lap. She was so engrossed in the story; she didn't notice me until I cleared my throat. Loudly.

"Oh, hey, Aster." She switched off the light so as not to waste the battery. We didn't need to see each other to talk, but she definitely needed to see to read. "I'm glad you're okay. We were all worried about you. Hugo made it seem like you were dead."

"Wishful thinking on his part." I joined her on the

ground. "Listen, there's something I've been meaning to talk to you about. Olive made an offer that I think you can't refuse."

"What kind of offer?"

"She needs a part-time worker at Olive Branch, and she has a spare room at her house for that lucky person." I looked at her. "She would like that lucky person to be you."

Hattie blanched. "Me? Why?"

"Because she thinks you're smart and young enough to learn, not like some of these old folks too stuck in their ways to change." I waved a hand in the direction of the campfire.

Hattie dropped her gaze to the book in her lap. "I'd work with books."

"And the cafe, too. Nike will probably need a bit of loving care."

"Cats don't generally like me, but Nike doesn't seem to mind," she said, more to herself.

"Nike's a good cat. And Olive's a good person. Salt of the earth, as my grandmother would say."

"I like Olive," she murmured.

"What's the problem?"

Hattie's face softened. "This is my crew, my family. I don't know that I want to leave you."

I squeezed her hand. "I get it, but this is an opportunity for you to have a better life. It's dangerous to be part of our group. We'll always be targets." And now I was a target with a name and a face. Things were poised to get a lot worse for us.

"I heard Bear and Scarlet talking about it. They can't believe the vampires didn't kill you when they had the chance."

"Sometimes life surprises us."

Hattie drew her knees closer to her chest. "Would you be upset if I decide to accept Olive's offer?"

"Upset? No, of course not. I'd miss you, but I also want what's best for you. Ours isn't a life I'd wish for anybody."

Hattie bit her lip. "It would be nice to have a toilet inside the house. I miss that."

I smiled. "I don't blame you. I miss that, too."

"You don't think her customers will mind that I'm a werewolf?"

"Why don't you pay her a visit and just have a conversation? Ask her your questions and then decide. There's no rush." Although the sooner Hattie was away from the hideout, the easier I'd sleep at night.

Hattie nodded slowly. "I can see myself there. I think I'd be happy."

I felt a pang of envy. I'd completely lost sight of what happiness looked like for me. It was all about survival and not much else. I wanted more for Hattie.

I patted her knee. "Let me know how it goes."

"Thank you, Aster. I don't care what Bonnie says, your heart isn't a cold brick wrapped in a glacier."

I resisted a smile. "Thanks, I appreciate the support."

I pushed myself to a standing position and returned to the campfire.

"Here she is," Bear said. "Ask her."

"Ask me what?" I lowered myself to a seated position.

Scarlet caught my eye. "How did you know the mob was coming?"

"I heard them," I said quickly. "They weren't exactly quiet."

"But you said you warned Doran while you were still inside. The fortress walls can't possibly be that thin."

"I don't understand why you warned him at all," Bonnie

said. "You should've let them run roughshod over everyone in there."

"Everyone in there would've included me," I pointed out. I couldn't bring myself to tell them the truth—not about my astral projection or my complicated feelings for Doran. They'd never understand.

"I don't know what we would've done if they'd killed you," Tyson interjected. "Without you, we're nothing."

"That's not true. Whether I'm here or not, you're a family." And while I was here, they were *my* family.

Scarlet glanced at Bonnie's protruding belly. "And pretty soon, we'll welcome a baby into this family."

"I hate to see Bonnie once her hormones start getting out of whack," Tyson said with a sly grin.

"What do you mean by starting?" Bear replied.

Bonnie elbowed him in the ribs.

"I'm just glad we're safe." Scarlet exhaled gently.

"I wouldn't describe any of us as safe," Bear objected. "Birney will want revenge. They know who Aster is now. They'll be posting her picture all over The Wild and offering a reward."

"But nearly everybody in The Wild already knows who I am." And the only one who'd betrayed me was Hugo.

Bear stared at me across the flames. "Mark my words. They'll up the ante high enough to tempt a weak villager. Security for a family might be worth far more than the occasional trinkets you toss at them. You're in more danger now than you ever were before. We're going to need to shore up our defenses."

I stared into the flames, losing myself in thought. Not only did Doran know my name and what I looked like, he also knew I possessed the power to kill him.

To kill them all.

* * *

Don't miss **Twilight Rebel**, the next book in the Midnight Empire: New Dawn trilogy.

To learn more about my books and join my VIP List to receive FREE bonus content, visit www.annabelchase.com.

Manufactured by Amazon.ca
Bolton, ON